D0277234

# A MERRY MISTRESS

# A MERRY MISTRESS

Judith Saxton

**Severn House Large Print**
London & New York

This first large print edition published in Great Britain 2004 by
SEVERN HOUSE LARGE PRINT BOOKS LTD of
9-15 High Street, Sutton, Surrey, SM1 1DF.
First world regular print edition published 2003 by
Severn House Publishers, London and New York.
This first large print edition published in the USA 2004 by
SEVERN HOUSE PUBLISHERS INC., of
595 Madison Avenue, New York, NY 10022.

Copyright © 1978 by Judy Turner
Introduction copyright © 2003 by Judith Saxton

All rights reserved.
The moral right of the author has been asserted.

British Library Cataloguing in Publication Data

Saxton,  Judith,  1936 -
    The merry mistress - Large print ed.
    1.  Gwyn, Nell, 1650–1687 – Fiction
    2.  Great Britain - History - Charles II,  1660 – 1685 - Fiction
    3.  Historical fiction
    4.  Large type books
    I.  Title  II. Turner, Judy, 1936-. Merry jade
    823.9'14 [F]

    ISBN 0-7278-7356-3

*For Auntie Elsie, Gill and Toni, who love the theatre.*

Except where actual historical events and characters are being
described for the storyline of this novel, all situations in this
publication are fictitious and any resemblance to living persons is
purely coincidental.

Printed and bound in Great Britain by
MPG Books Ltd, Bodmin, Cornwall.

*For Auntie Elsie, Gill and Toni,*
*who love the theatre.*

# Introduction

When writing historical novels it is tempting to choose great figures of the past, but I usually concentrated on the less well known since I found their lives more interesting. I decided to investigate Nell Gwyn after reading a particularly cruel and critical novel about her, written by a man, and soon decided she was much maligned.

She was as pretty and witty as her contemporaries said, but she was sweet-natured and generous too; unless one was a court lady one did not rise to be the King's mistress by being haughty or horrible. So I set out to put the record straight as I saw it...

(c) 2003 by Judith Saxton

# Acknowledgements

I would like to thank the staff of the Wrexham library for their cheerful, never-failing help; and also John Grundy of Glan Garth, Wrexham, for the loan of some of his invaluable reference books.

# One

The sun was setting over London. Between the tall houses by the river, the golden rays slanted across green grass, gilded the skeletal branches of trees, and brought its brilliance to sparkle on every ripple of the great river. But down in the slum streets off Drury Lane, so closely huddled were the mean houses that night, here, had already come. In Lewknor Lane, a small girl standing well back in the shadow of a doorway looked apprehensively up at the sky, and was relieved to see no stars yet pricked its deep blue brilliance. It could not be night yet, then, which was as well, for she must not be here too late.

She was a small, thin child, clad in a threadbare shawl which covered her from the top of her head to her knee; below the knees her bare, dirty legs ended in bare, dirty feet. She was trying to stand still, to blend into the shadows of the doorway in which she stood, but every now and again, almost despite herself, her cold toes scuffled in the filth, as though seeking, in vain, for warmth.

She took little notice of the passersby, for it was not from them that her release would come. They were a furtive, mean looking crowd for the most part, though every now and then a small knot of gentlemen, be-wigged and wearing the silks and satins of the court, would swagger past. In the gutter, a drunk rolled. His unrepentant singing and bawling had faded into silence now, and he lay quiet, save for an occasional moan or belch. The child had watched him tolerantly enough, for she did not fear him, nor find his condition frightening or rare. Plainly, drunken men were as much a part of her life as was the ragged shawl which she clutched around her.

It was on the doorway directly opposite her that the child's attention was focussed. Several times the door had swung open, but always people entered, no-one came out.

But now, the door opened, spilling a sliver of golden candlelight onto the pavement, and a young woman emerged. She huddled a shawl around her, shivering in the keen evening air, and set off at a sharp walk along the pavement, pressing close to the mean houses, as anxious as the child that she should not be noticed.

'Rose!' The child ran across the roadway, not heeding the dirt which splashed up at her from the kennel, nor the drunk in the gutter, who cursed and clutched at her shadow as it fled across his face. 'Rose! Wait for me, I've come to see you home safe.'

The older girl swung round, hand to mouth, and then smiled down at the child, her face softening with relief.

'Nellie! Bless my soul if it isn't our Nell! But what are you doing here, at this time of night? There are bad people about, you know that well! You oughtn't to be here!'

'No one notices me; that's the good part of being small,' the child said composedly, slipping her hand into her sister's ready clasp. 'You'd never think I was eleven, would you, Rose? An' I come for you 'acos you said to Ma how afraid you were of the dark streets, and the drunks, an' such. I thought two would be safer than one, anyhow.'

'But I didn't mean for you to come,' Rose protested. 'I thought Ma might – she's quick enough to grab my money when I'm paid – but I s'pose she didn't want to put herself out.'

'She had a man in,' Nell explained. 'Not but what she wouldn't have come anyway. Likes to settle down with her feet up of an evening, does Ma.'

Her sister nodded, and for a moment they walked in silence, intent upon their own thoughts. Neither would have condemned for one moment their mother's occasional prostitution. It brought an element of comfort into their hard lives, for the money she made from her more regular employment as a fruit seller in the nearby market did little besides paying the rent and providing basic necessities such as bread and ale. Their father had died so many years before that they could scarcely remember him, though Rose had a vague recollection of a lusty, red-haired man who came into the dingy kitchen on a great bellow of laughter, and had made even the dirty cottage in Coal Yard seem a brighter place. But that had been long ago, when Nell was a tiny baby. Their father had gone to fight for the King across the water, as they called King Charles the second then, and had been killed, whether in England, or in France, or in Holland, even, was never made clear to them.

Their mother, Mrs Ellen Gwyn, must have been a pretty girl, once. She was still pretty in a blowsy, over-ripe way, with faded yellow hair, a cushiony figure, and a great capacity for drink and laughter. Easy-going she certainly was, and generous, once her own needs had been provided for. When she made money she spent it as freely on her daughters as on herself, and now, as they pushed open the cottage door and stepped into the low-ceilinged, dark little kitchen, she looked up from her position of lazy comfort, to say, 'Rabbit stew for supper!' as she wriggled the fat, bare legs held out to the blaze, and held up her skirts the better to enjoy the warmth of the fire.

'Rabbit stew! Oh, I love it,' Rose declared, heading for the firelight like a moth to the flame. 'Fanny gave me a piece of white sugar to suck, coming home, but Nell and I have been so busy, chattering that I forgot it. Here, we can use it,' and she threw the piece of sugar loaf onto the table with a clatter.

'And I bought a pile of little apples off the stall,' Mrs Gwyn said triumphantly, 'which can be cooked up quick as a trice. My, what a dinner!'

'About time we had a decent meal,' Nell said cheekily, tipping Rose a wink. 'Here's Rosie, working like a skivvy, and me, toiling at the housework, and what sort of food do we get? Leavings and pickings!'

'I do well by you,' Mrs Gwyn grumbled, but without malice. She jingled her apron pocket suggestively. 'I meant to bake, but this feller took a fancy to come home wi' me, and now I've a bit of money in the kitty. He gave me an idea, too, this feller. I told him I'd a pair of daughters, and he said he'd come a-visiting some time with some friends of his. No use for *you*, Nellie, but Rose is growing up to be a fine little wench. You've got to lose your virtue some time, gal, and the feller said his friend would pay well for it. You could buy yourself some real pretty gowns and gew-gaws.'

'But who would want me, when they'd seen the beauties at Madam Ross's house?' Rose said practically. 'A new one came in to day, Ma, and she's the prettiest yet! The longest curling golden hair, great blue eyes, and the tiniest hands and feet. But you should hear her swear!' She chuckled at the recollection. 'A nobleman who visits the house came in, and caught her arm, and she pulled away and his hand ripped her lace. Blinded him up hill and down dale for ten minutes, she did!'

'I think you're pretty,' Nell said stoutly. '*And* you can swear good, Rose! Why don't you go with the ladies at Madam's, instead of being made to do all the work?'

'You've not seen the girls, or you wouldn't ask,' Rose said. 'Is the stew nearly ready, Ma? I'm starved!'

'Just about,' Mrs Gwyn said, heaving herself reluctantly to her feet. 'Get the bowls out, Nellie, there's a good gal. And Rose, I mean what I say. We'll be better off, a deal, if you go out from here rather than from Ross's. And as for what you've got that Madam's girls haven't, why, your virginity, you foolish creature! Tomorrow we'll wash

17

your hair under the pump, and I'll buy you a new gown. You see, when you're cleaned up a bit you'll be grand!'

'What about me, then?' Nell said, trotting over to the table with three wooden bowls. 'Shall I get a new gown? It's about time!'

'A *new* one? When you've not got a gown to your back?' Rose said, laughing. She tweaked the shawl round Nell's shoulders and it fell off, revealing that the child's skinny body was naked save for a grubby petticoat, ragged edged, which lacked one sleeve and most of the back.

'Stop that!' Nell said sharply, re-wrapping her small person. 'Why shouldn't I have a gown, then? The more reason, as I've not got one at all!'

'To own the truth, I think you should have a gown,' Mrs Gwyn agreed, ladling the stew carefully into the dishes before her. She gestured with the spoon. 'Bring up the stools girls, and Rosie, cut a hunk off of that loaf. Yes, Nell, you must have a gown, even if it is only Rose's old blue one. For I shall send you to Madam, in place of Rose. How will you like that, eh?'

'She'll never have me,' Nell said gloomily.

'She'll say I'm too young.'

'Perhaps, in the ordinary way. But if you go round tomorrow and say you've come to do your sister's work, because she is sick, then it'll be a different story.' Mrs Gwyn beamed at them, pleased with her own guile. 'There, what about that, eh?'

'It *might* work,' Rose admitted. 'Madam's that lazy, and it would save her sending out for another girl, or doing the work herself. And you'd get some money too, Nell.'

'Can I keep some of it, though?' Nell asked suspiciously. She bent over her plate and sniffed ecstatically. 'Wish we had rabbit stew *every* day, and stewed apple after. If I can keep some of the money, I'll buy us good things to eat with it!'

'Keep money? You'd not know what to do with it,' her mother scoffed, tearing off a piece of bread and dipping it into the gravy. She blew on it, then popped it into her mouth. 'I'm a devilish fine cook when I put my mind to it,' she remarked thickly. 'Then we're agreed? You shall both have a good scrubbing tomorrow morning, early, and Nellie shall go to Madam's in the blue gown. Rose shall stay indoors whilst I get

19

her something pretty to wear and then we'll wait to see if my feller comes back, with his friend who will pay high for a virgin.'

'How high?' Nell asked curiously. She noticed that her sister had stopped eating and was toying with her spoon, whilst the bright colour flooded her face until even her forehead was stained with pink.

'He said five golden guineas if the girl was comely and willing, and if he was sure he was first there,' Mrs Gwyn said grudgingly, 'But whether he'll *really* pay so much...' she sighed, and then grinned suddenly. 'Wish I'd a dozen daughters,' she said. 'How about your friend Sal? Would she like me to find her a buyer?'

'She lost her maidenhead when she was twelve, to one of those freckled Campbell boys,' Rose said, recovering her countenance and beginning to eat once more. 'Lucky for you, Ma, that I started work young and saw too much at Madam's to want to play dirty with the boys.'

Her mother chuckled. 'Aye. And you don't mind goin' with the young man from here, do you? Only you're getting so pretty that one of these days someone at Ross's will take you for one of the ladies, instead of just a servant. And you'd not get a penny piece out of it.'

'No, I don't mind,' Rose said, helping herself to another piece of bread. 'And if Nellie keeps my job warm then I can go back there if I find the gentlemen don't fancy me after all.'

The scrubbing had worked miracles on Rose, Nell considered, as she trudged up Lewknor Lane, her heart bumping in her thin chest. After their combined shrieks had been quenched temporarily by the torrents of water, Rose had emerged as just the sort of pink and gold beauty her mother had envisaged. Her hair had dried naturally curly and as yellow as the day-old chicks sold down at the market, and her skin glow-ed with scrubbing and health. Despite her words, Mrs Gwyn had not sent Nell off to Ross's immediately, but had let Rose don the old gown and go down to Mrs Fitch on the market, who sold secondhand clothes. Rose had chosen well, a gown of soft blue which matched her eyes and a piece of blue satin ribbon to thread through her curls.

Nell had finally hurried off to her new job leaving Rose sitting on their front door step, talking self-consciously to the young Arny Brett, whose face reflected his astonishment at the change wrought by soap and water.

Lewknor Lane in the early afternoon did not look as fearsome as it had done in the dusk, but the daylight showed up the dirt and the forlorn aspect of Madam Ross's, and the absence of welcoming candlelight made it seem grim and forbidding, so that Nell, despite herself, hesitated. But then she remembered the change wrought in her own appearance by the scrubbing and the faded blue gown, and straightened her shoulders. She approached the front door, which was half-open, and hesitated, wondering whether to knock, when her problem was solved for her. In the shaft of light which fell through the door and onto the stairs sat a pretty girl, mending the flounce of a petticoat.

'Hello, ducks!' The girl said cheerfully. She stretched and yawned, showing a rent under the sleeve of her soiled pink gown. 'Got a message, 'ave you?'

'Yes. Well, that is...' stammered Nell, 'Me

sister Rose works here, but she's ill and Ma sent me to tell Madam I'd do Rose's work for a day or so.'

The girl eyed her shrewdly. 'Thought Rose 'ud be taking off on her own soon,' she said. 'Rose Gwyn's your sister, eh? Well, I don't say she's wrong to get some good out of herself from her first man, but after that she might as well come back to Madam's. At least we're not on the streets, and now that the King's come into his own again, we get a good class of customer.'

'She thinks she isn't pretty enough,' Nell explained, hearing the slight frost in the girl's tone and correctly concluding that it would not do to let anyone believe Rose had scorned Madam's establishment. 'She's only fourteen, you know.'

'Well, that's true,' said the girl, mollified. 'Not but what I've thought lately that with a good wash and a clean gown, Rose could hold her own with most. And how old are you, dearie? Nine? Ten?'

'Almost twelve,' Nell said. 'Do you suppose Madam will let me do Rose's work?'

'Face her with a fact and she'll not turn you out. So I'll show you what to do, and you must make a decent job of it. By the way, I'm Fanny Kelly. Perhaps Rose has mentioned me.'

'Very often,' Nell said. 'You gave her a gown once, a brown silk, with the richest lace!'

'Aye, that's right. But it didn't suit her.' Fanny looked consideringly at Nell's long, auburn hair and sparkling redbrown eyes. 'It would have looked well on you. I suppose it has gone long since?'

'Yes. It was sold to buy this blue one that I'm wearing.'

'Aye, but it doesn't fit you, that blue gown. If you've time when you've finished your work I'll show you how to alter a gown to fit you,' Fanny said. She finished her work, bit off her cotton, and stood up. 'Come on little ... what's your name? Nell? Come on then, Nell, and I'll put you into the way of things. First, you must clean the room where the gentlemen wait to meet the girls. And then you'd best help Mrs Fletcher with the suppers, for you're a bit late and by now most of the girls will have done their own rooms. Rose didn't usually stay on to serve the customers with drink, did she?'

Nell shook her head. Rose had often bewailed the fact, for sometimes the men would tip a serving wench and if the girls were lucky with their lovers, presents were occasionally forthcoming.

'No. Well, dear, your sister wasn't overly clean,' Fanny said. 'But you've given yourself a good scrubbing and your gown can soon be altered. If nothing's said, you just come with me and begin to hand round supper and drinks. You'll be a bit late home, but it will ensure Madam's keeping you on. She'll see she's got a rare bargain!'

When Nell set off in the direction of Coal Yard again, it was after midnight. She was tired, but her heart was high, for she carried a little purse with coins clinking within. And her gown fitted her neatly, and the shawl around her shoulders was a new one, soft and grey as smoke.

The day's work had been successful and she had enjoyed serving the gentlemen, quickly becoming neat and efficient at weaving her way between the chairs and the small groups of bargaining, laughing men and women. Madam Ross, a big boned, elderly woman with a mouth like a rattrap, had proved surprisingly willing to employ Nell. She had looked around at the work the girl had done, and then watched closely as Nell handed suppers and drinks, noting her bright, unselfconscious smile and her quick witted repartee. 'Come at the same time in the morning,' was all she had said, but Fanny Kelly had slipped out into the corridor when Rose had been at last dismissed, and had given her young friend the purse. 'Madam's pleased with you, and several of the men put their hands in their pockets,' she said. 'Don't be late in the morning, ducks!'

So now Nell approached the cottage in Coal Yard with excitement, knowing that she had good news to impart. She pushed open the door and slipped inside. The fire was in, but only just, and Rose was lying on their pallet before it, her wide eyes fixed on the glowing ashes.

'It's me, Rose, I'm back,' Nell said. She felt the tiredness lift from her and ran across the room, flopping down on the pallet beside her sister. 'Look, Madam let me serve the gentlemen, which is why I'm late, and I've got all this *money*, and Fanny Kelly altered my gown to fit, and I'm to work there every day!' Something about her sister's silence made her turn her head, gazing enquiringly at the older girl. 'What about you, Rose? Did he come?'

Rose didn't speak, but she held out her hand. In the pale glow from the dying fire, Nell saw in the shadows on her sister's palm the glint of gold.

# Two

'Ma! Rosie!'

Nell flung herself into the kitchen and came to a halt in the middle of the room, her breath still coming short with the exertion of running, but her face bright with excitement. Rose and Mrs Gwyn, shelling peas at the square wooden table, looked up enquiringly.

'I am to go to the King's Theatre, at Drury Lane, as an orange girl! The work is quite hard, but the money is good, especially if you please the gentlemen. And best of all, I shall see all the plays free, and be near...' she faltered, then concluded 'Near the actors and actresses,' in an unconvincing voice.

'Near Charlie Hart you mean,' Rose said accusingly, but with some amusement. 'You fell for the chap the first time you saw him on stage, and well I know it. But as for

28

seeing the plays, Nell, how can you? Orange girls have their backs to the stage so that they can spot their customers. If you start facing away from the audience you'll not make much money.'

'Don't worry, I shan't lose any customers,' Nell said airily. She dropped her shawl on the nearest stool and taking a handful of peas, began to shell them into the saucepan. 'It just shows that it pays to keep clean and work hard, and to stick to your friends. Who would have thought that Fanny Kelly's latest lover could encompass such a thing, though? And me her best friend for three years now, so that when he mentioned Orange Moll wanting a girl, mine was the first name that dear Fanny thought of!'

Rose glanced at her sister. A small girl still, with sherry coloured hair falling in soft, natural waves down to her waist. Her figure was boylike, save for tiny budding breasts, yet she was totally feminine, from her big lively eyes to her pointed little chin.

'Fanny's lover could not have got you the job unless you had been right for it,' Rose said now.

'Well, let's hope the money's good,' Mrs

Gwyn observed. She popped the last pod, ran the peas into the pan, and picked it up by the handle. 'I'll just draw some water,' she said, and left the kitchen.

Rose raised enquiring eyebrows at her sister. She no longer lived at home, though she was a frequent visitor, and she knew that with every passing year her mother grew lazier. With both her daughters present it seemed strange that she should have gone out to pump water.

'She's got a bottle hid,' Nell said briefly. 'No use to chase her. All I can do is see that she doesn't find my money. I give her some, and she buys our food and some of our clothes. But what she earns for herself sometimes goes on drink.'

'Sometimes?'

Nell grinned and her dimples sprang into being, making Rose smile back at her. 'Oh, don't worry, she has to pay the rent, and coal, and bread. Her money from the stall goes on that. It's just that when she brings a man home now, she spends the money on brandy. I've given up trying to stop her. It's her greatest pleasure, you see. But I made it plain that not a penny of mine would go that way, and that I wouldn't start paying for the rent and that out of my earnings.'

'You've got more courage than I had at thirteen,' Rose said with a shrug. 'How many other orange girls did they take on? Anyone I know?'

'Only me,' Nell said, triumphantly. 'They'd only the one place, you see. As soon as I went in I told the woman – a Mrs Clarke it was – that I'd been sent by Mr Stennet, who thought I might be what she was looking for, and she just sort of sniffed. But then another girl came in with a basket of oranges she'd bought at the market. It was Lizzy Campbell, remember her? I chaffed her over the price she'd paid, and she chaffed me over my gown, and the old girl listened with her head on one side. Then she just said, 'Think you can buy your fruit cheaper, eh?' So I explained I was only teasing Lizzy, but that my ma works for Dobman on a market stall so I usually get good prices. And she said, 'Right, you should do. You're hired.'

'And then?'

'Oh well, she looked at me for a moment, and said, 'Have you got a pretty gown? In green?' I said I had, which is true, Rose, for you know that Fanny gave me a green gown a while back, and it still fits me. And then she said go home, put the green gown on, give your hair a good brush and be back for two o'clock.'

'You'll see all the courtiers, because the King and his brother, the Duke, often go to the play,' Rose said thoughtfully. 'What about Madam Ross though, Nell? You could keep on your job there, I should think. After all, you're free from about six o'clock, and Madam's business is only starting then.'

'That's true,' Nell said. 'But if I do, when shall I shop, and keep an eye on Ma? I'm supposed to go mornings to the theatre, too, because of rehearsals. Not every day, mind, but most days.'

'If you're going to earn good money, it might be best if you left Ma and Coal Yard altogether, and turned respectable,' Rose said. 'I left, didn't I? I had to! What with Ma drunk, and dirty most of the time, and taking every penny from me, I'd have gone under, else.'

'She's better now,' Nell said defensively. 'What would she do if I left? Drink herself to death, probably. No, it would be different if I was living with a man, like you are with young Braithwaite. I know you couldn't have Ma living with you, because no man would stand for it. But I can cope with her.'

'If you change your mind, come to see me and I'll help you get lodgings,' Rose promised. She had been sitting beside the table, absently opening the empty pods and chewing the sweet ones, but now she got to her feet and crossed over to the oven, hollowed out of the wall beside the fire. 'There's a meat and potato pie in here, heating through. If Ma doesn't hurry with those peas, the pie'll be done to a turn and there'll be nothing to eat with it. Shall you go and call her, or shall I?'

She took her big basket of oranges on her arm that first time, and crept into the theatre. Such a vast, opulent place it seemed, with scores of candles illumining the pit where the orange girls stood to sell their wares, and the benches already crowded with spectators. The play was *Othello* and the actress playing Desdemona had a large following, as did Charles Hart, who played the Moor, so naturally the play was well-attended. Standing next to Lizzy Campbell, wildly excited by the babble of voices, the colour of the court dresses, and the air of tenseness and excitement emanating from the stage, Nell found herself scanning the faces of the audience, looking for someone, anyone, whom she might know. Many of the women were masked, making identification difficult, as indeed it was meant to, but Nell recognised Fanny Kelly, sitting with a friend.

Fanny, glancing around her, recognised Nell at the same moment and waved. Nell waved back but Lizzy nudged her sharply in the ribs. 'When someone waves to you, you must run across with your basket before one of the other girls does,' she hissed. 'You won't get customers coming to you, you know!'

Nell obediently trotted across to Fanny's bench, trying to make the heavy basket seem light. 'Yes, Madam?' She said brightly, barely suppressing a giggle. On closer inspection, Fanny looked so different in her stiff and starched best gown, with her golden ringlets neatly combed instead of flowing freely around her face.

But Fanny said seriously, 'You look the part, Nellie. Shall you be at the house to-night?'

'Aye,' Nell said, holding out her hand for the money as Fanny picked two oranges out of her basket. 'It seems that I can do both jobs. And the money is always useful.'

'That's true, but you may find a better position, from here,' Fanny said, nodding. 'We're here to see the play of course, but who knows? We might find ourselves some business as well, eh, Sally?'

The slim, dark haired girl sitting masked, next to her, said 'We might indeed,' and Nell recognised one of the more successful of Madam's girls. The innocent look and air was part of her charm, but it hid the nature of a virago, as Nell knew to her cost. Many a time she had hurled a missile at Nell, blaming her for a badly made bed or for a torn cuff, neither of which would have been anyone's fault but Sal's. But Sally was popular with the men so the other girls tolerated her, making sure that when Sally's temper flew out of the window, they themselves flew out of the nearest door!

However, she was on her best behaviour tonight and smiled kindly at Nell as she curtsied and left them. And as if her first sale had been a signal, a hand reached out to tug her skirt as she made her way back to the pit. 'Over here, maid,' a voice urged. 'What's your name? Nell? Well, I'll have half-a-dozen oranges, Nellie.'

By the time the performance started, Nell's basket was light and her pocket satisfactorily heavy, for she had sold quite half her wares. But despite her resolve not to watch the stage too closely, Nell found herself unable to resist turning every time Desdemona took the stage. The actress taking the part was beautiful, with dark hair and eyes and very white skin, but it was not her looks which brought Nell's head round every time she came onto the stage.

It was her acting, and her voice. A deep voice for a woman, but so musical was it, so full of expression, that Nell felt she could have listened all night. Even Charles Hart, whose dark good looks had won her deepest admiration the first time ever she had been to the theatre, could not hold her attention as Desdemona was doing.

At last the play finished, the last of the oranges were sold, and the girls began to make their way out of the theatre. Fanny had indeed found the 'business' she had hoped for, and had left with a young man, but Nell walked with Lizzy and they chattered their way back to Coal Yard.

'I thought the woman who was Desdemona was wonderful,' Nell said. 'She's got such a lovely voice.'

'Yes, that was Peg Hughes, a very important actress,' Lizzy informed her friend. 'She lives with a lord, they say. When she isn't acting, I mean.'

'I wish I could be an actress,' Nell said wistfully. 'I'd love to walk across the stage, wringing my hands and weeping, or wearing a pretty gown and making folk laugh. But I suppose I'm not pretty enough.'

'I don't think prettiness counts for much,' Lizzy said. 'You've got to read, for a start. And speak real nicely, like Peg Hughes does.'

'Oh!' Nell said, rather startled. 'Read? I suppose so. And I'd like to talk proper...ly! I reckon I could do that. But read?'

'How else can you learn your parts?' Lizzy

said practically. 'Can't say I'm interested. If you play your cards right, in the pit, you can have any man you fancy. And if you get a regular keeper, with money, you're made!'

'I'd rather be an actress, and not need the men,' Nell said obstinately. 'But to learn to read! Who'd teach me?'

'Who indeed? Better forget it, for who would take up an orange girl?'

Nell's shoulders drooped for a moment, then straightened resolutely. 'I'll find someone.'

Despite her resolve, it was a little while before Nell did find someone to help with her reading, and then the help came from an unexpected quarter. Another orange girl, Betty Ball, started soon after Nell, and the two quickly became good friends, for they had one thing in common; both wanted to be actresses.

They were both bright, intelligent girls, quick with a pert answer, and soon became favourites with the theatre-going crowd, but it did not seem that their efforts to learn to read were to be crowned with success. Together, whilst the players rehearsed, Betty and Nell would try to follow the dialogue on stage in a copy of the play which they would borrow from an actor who already knew his role. But it was uphill work, with no-one to correct their mistakes or explain their errors.

And then, one morning, luck smiled upon them. They were sitting in their usual place, in one of the benches in the front row, holding a copy of the play between them. Betty's dark head with its thickly curling crop and Nell's coppery one were close together, making an arresting contrast. It may have been that which brought them to Thomas Killigrew's notice. He stepped down from the stage, motioning the players to carry on without him and walked, soft-footed, over to the two girls.

'This word *must* be "sir", from what they've just said,' Nell was saying. 'Oh, Bet, if only someone could just help us a little, I'm sure we would soon understand!'

'Help you with what?' The voice so close made Nell jump, and Betty jumped too, and between them they dropped the book.

Killigrew smiled at them. 'I see you're learning to read,' he said. 'Well done! It's something you'll never regret, for it opens the world of books and plays to you. You can read six books during the run of one play, imagine that!'

The builder, manager and guiding spirit behind the theatre was a man to be stared at with awe by two little orange girls; to be spoken to by him was a wonderful thing which left Betty gaping. But Nell saw an opportunity and jumped at it. As he turned to go she tugged at his sleeve. 'It's too difficult alone, sir,' she said urgently. 'Me and Bet want to be actresses, but how can we do that if we can't read? Can you not help us?'

Killigrew glanced indulgently down at the two hopeful faces turned up to his. 'There is bound to be someone. Ask the players,' he said. And then, abruptly, 'What play are you reading?'

'The Parson's Wedding, which is in rehearsal,' Nell said promptly, knowing that Killigrew had written the play himself. 'Or we would be reading it, if we could, sir.'

He had been on the point of turning from them once more, but the reply arrested him and he gave a rueful laugh. 'Well, at least you've good taste! I'll try to arrange for someone to help you both.'

'He never will,' Betty said gloomily as Killigrew rejoined the actors on stage with a cry of 'Children, children, you must listen to each other as well as to me! Turn this way, Theo, when Ann is speaking.'

Nell's eyes sparkled. 'If he does not then we must remind him!'

But there was no need to remind him. Next day, as the two of them struggled with a primer which they had acquired, Peg Hughes herself came up to them.

'Mistress Gwyn? Mistress Ball?' she asked solemnly, though her eyes twinkled. 'At Mr Killigrew's request, I am to give you a reading lesson.'

She proved to be a delightful teacher; not so very much older than them, after all, and a patient, good-natured creature. When the other players saw Peg Hughes helping them, they offered help too, even Charles Hart condescending to spend an hour with them sometimes, and everyone showed genuine pleasure at their increasing proficiency.

One day, Nell was by herself in Peg Hughes' dressing room. She was hemming a flounced petticoat, for she loved Peg and could not do enough for her. Stitching away, she sat on Peg's round velvet stool dreaming of the day she would be on the stage herself, and would dazzle and enchant the audience as Peg did. Often, from her lowly position in the pit, Nell would look up and see the King himself watching one or other of the actresses with more than casual interest. She liked the King. He was not nearly so handsome as Charles Hart, but his dark, rather sad eyes were kind, and there was something about him which attracted her, though she was too young to know precisely what. Sometimes he called to her, pretending that he wanted to buy oranges, but he would slip a billet into her basket, smiling knowingly at her, over-paying for the oranges, so that she would deliver it to the lady of his choice.

He is a lovely man, for all he's ugly, she was thinking to herself as she switched. But I would not lie with him; he wants too much variety and when I have a man I want him to be mine alone. I want him to buy me pretty things, and kiss me and fuss me, and love only me out of the whole wide world!

Abruptly, her pleasant reverie was shattered by the door bursting open. Hart strode

into the room, shouting 'Peg!' in an out-
raged roar. Nell, jumping to her feet, said
reproachfully, 'You didn't ought to bellow
like that, sir. You gave me the most terrible
fright, and Mistress Hughes won't be here
for an hour or more, you know that.'

'Oh, it's you, Nellie,' Hart growled. 'I only
hope Peg does turn up. You know what she's
like – no, I suppose you don't, on second
thoughts. She enjoys tragic and dramatic
roles, and she works hard in 'em, but when
we turn to comedy, or when her lover
beckons, there's no thought for us! Oh no,
then Mistress Margaret packs her things
and moves out!'

'But this play's not run its course yet,' Nell
reminded him. 'And Peg's left all her things
here. So what *has* put you in such a stew?'

'Cheeky wench,' Hart said without rancour. 'I know the play's not finished, but
Sedley's gone to Newmarket to see about
buying some horses. If Peg goes with him,
who will speak her part?'

'Ann Marshall? She could, she's little to
say in this play,' volunteered Nell.

'Aye, but she's a slow study,' grumbled
Hart. 'Tell you what, Nellie, you want to be

43

an actress, don't you? Why don't you learn the main parts as they come along? It would be good practice for you, and you never know when your chance might come.'

Nell put down her work and eyed Hart suspiciously. 'Would I get paid?' She asked.

'Aye. I'd give you lessons in acting when I'd the time, and so would the others,' Hart said promptly. 'And you never know, you might fall into one of the chief parts, through the player leaving, or falling ill.'

'But how can I go straight from being an orange girl in the pit to taking a main part?' Nell said, not to be sidetracked by dreams of glory from the hard facts of life. 'I have to buy my fruit, and clean it and arrange it, and I work at Madam Ross's, handing the suppers and cleaning.'

'Tell Orange Moll to find herself another wench to sell oranges,' Hart said recklessly. 'I'll see you get some stage experience, Nellie! You can do walk-ons, then tiny speaking parts, and then when your big moment comes you'll be ready to face it, and show 'em all!'

Nell bounced on the balls of her feet, her face flooding with delicate colour. 'Before

God, Mr Hart, it is what I've longed for most! Are you *sure*?'

'Certain,' he confirmed. He put his arm round her narrow shoulders, giving them a slight squeeze, and Nell exuberantly hugged him back. He turned to look at her with more attention. 'You're so tiny though, girl! Yet with that lovely colouring, and your clear voice, I think you'll make it to the top, one day.'

'I will, I will!' Nell said recklessly, casting doubts aside for later. 'But what about Betty? She's been learning to read alongside me, Mr Hart.'

'It wouldn't do to rob Orange Moll of two of her girls,' Hart objected. 'Besides, she's not come on as quickly as you, Nellie. The last time you read to me – Tuesday, wasn't it? – you'd not only got the reading off pat, you were coming on nicely with expression and accent, and that's something that some people never learn.'

'I hope I don't lose my friend,' Nell said. Then excitement overcame her scruples. 'But Bet won't bear a grudge because I'm the first picked out,' she said. 'And don't think I don't know what salary I shall be

45

getting, because I do!'

Betty lived up to her friend's expectations for she bore no grudge, though her envy was abundant. 'Did Mr Hart not ask anything of you, in return for the favour?' She said curiously. 'He's a fine man, and I'd not mind obliging him in bed one little bit – quite the opposite, in fact!'

'No, he didn't,' Nell said, feeling almost ashamed to make the admission. 'But I'll not be fourteen for a while yet. A bit young for a mistress, perhaps.'

'And you don't look thirteen, even,' Betty said seriously. 'You could easily act the part of a boy, Nell, for you've not got much figure yet.'

'Oh, that will come,' Nell said hopefully. 'My sister Rose was small for her age, but she grew bigger and plumper when she became fourteen. She's quite tall and buxom now!'

'What will your Ma say?'

'I'll tell you tomorrow,' Nell said, skipping towards the door.

# Three

'If you don't put some flesh on, Nellie, folk will take you for a lad off the stage as well as on,' Mrs Gwyn grumbled. It struck Nell, not for the first time, that since she had become one of the King's players, Mrs Gwyn had done more than her fair share of grumbling about this and that.

She was sitting by the fire, making over a gown given by one of the Queen's maids of honour, Frances Stewart. Unfortunately, she was quite a foot taller than Nell, so all the gorgeous, richly worked garments which she passed on so generously had to be extensively altered before Nell could wear them.

'If you'd a man to keep you, you would be able to buy your gowns new, instead of straining your eyes altering the stuff the King's piece hands on to you,' Mrs Gwyn said spitefully.

Nell sighed, but did not reply. She had heard all the arguments before. Why, her mother asked, had not Charles Hart taken her to his bed? Or if he was not interested, why did she not accept the offers made by the young bucks who haunted the stage more from an interest in the actresses than in the plays? The answer, that Hart and the other players had no desire to see their leading comedy actress grow fat and pregnant so that she could no longer delight audiences with her impersonations of young men, did not satisfy Mrs Gwyn.

And to be truthful, Nell knew that her own burning ambition to make good on the stage kept her out of the beds of men who would have welcomed her presence in their lives. She simply *must* make a name for herself before she became any man's mistress. Hart, John Lacy, Theo Bird, Nick Burt and the others all urged her to remain true to the stage until her reputation was assured.

'If you fool with a man, and get pregnant, your career will end with the child's swelling your belly,' Hart told her earnestly. 'You'll be taken eagerly enough, for although you're only a child yet, some of the courtiers would welcome the novelty of that, and you're pretty and famous. But then they'd cast you off and you'd find the theatre a hard mistress, for there is always an actress to replace a lass who's not yet firmly fixed as a name in the mind of audiences.'

'If you'd take a keeper, we could move into decent lodgings,' Mrs Gwyn continued fretfully. 'If it wasn't for Rosie slipping a few coins into my hand now and then, I'd be in a poor way. Not a decent gown to my back but the rubbish you alter to fit me, nor a bit of pleasure but what you grudgingly allow me.'

'If I'd a man to keep me, he wouldn't keep you,' Nell reminded her placidly. 'And if I gave you money you'd be drunk all the time, instead of nine-tenths of the time. You're only annoyed because I won't let you drink yourself to death, you old fool.'

Mrs Gwyn grinned suddenly. 'Talking to your Ma like that! Eh, but I shouldn't nag you, Nell, for you don't do so bad by me. And God knows, I've no desire to dandle a grandchild on my knee. I suppose you're afraid the theatre would turn you off whilst you were making the child?'

'That, and because I won't take second place for the rest of my life,' Nell said, finishing a seam and getting to her feet. 'I've done this now, Ma, and I'd best be off. We've a rehearsal this morning, and Mr Hart likes me to arrive in good time. No performance this afternoon, though, so Becky Marshall and I are going to slum it at the Duke's House. They're doing 'Mustapha', and Moll Davies is playing the Queen of Hungary. And Roxalana is taken by Eliza Davenport, who is being kept by the Earl of Oxford. Imagine him letting his mistress go back to the stage, just like that!'

But the remark, as it turned out, was an unfortunate one. 'Yes, and *you* could be in such circumstances if you could just but forget your high and mighty ways,' Mrs Gwyn said ominously, recalling her grievance. 'Don't try to tell me different! Betty comes round here with her black eyes wide, full of tales about the men who want you. Titled, rich, the lot. And the presents they'd pour out on you, the fine lodgings! But do you listen to your old Ma? Do you let me advise you? The one who...'

But Nell never discovered what her mother was now claiming to have done for her, because she slipped quietly out of the door and set off along Drury Lane in the direction of the Marshall sisters' lodgings. She and her mother had moved out of Coal Yard several months before, and at first Mrs Gwyn had been enchanted by her lovely new home. But it had not lasted. Disillusion set in as soon as she realised her daughter had no intention of increasing their income still further by sleeping with the men who thronged about her. And now, Nell was seriously considering moving away from her present lodgings up to the other, more fashionable end of the Lane. She would continue to pay her mother's rent, of course, and to see that she was fed; but she would not have to suffer the annoyance of the men her mother still occasionally brought in, or of her continual plaint that she was being starved of the smallest pleasures in life by her ungrateful daughter.

Her friend's lodging was near her own, but she did not have to walk even that far, because Rebecca came to meet her, running down the road with her skirt flying back to reveal a petticoat so pretty and so ruched, embroidered and edged with lace that Nell felt a pang of envy, and a momentary regret for her own attire. But Becky, without preamble, said frankly, 'You look so nice, Nell! I wish I had your colouring, and then I could wear naught but green and white, and look crisp and elegant! As it is, I strain my eyes over bunching the lace richly, and still cannot attain the air which you have. Oh, and you've new shoes! Those big buckles make your feet look even smaller.'

'It's a good thing I *do* look nice in simple clothes,' Nell said a trifle moodily. 'For if I move away from Ma then I shall have two rents to pay. But it might be worth it for a bit of peace.'

'You could always earn some more money, after the play finishes,' Becky said slyly. 'I got this petticoat from Mr Selborne, and a beautiful gown in wine red velvet. And he paid my lodging rent for a month, too.'

'And one day you'll find yourself pregnant, and Mr Selborne will swear he's not the father, because you got your previous month's rent from your friend Collier, and he'll say it might have been Howard, because he bought you shoes with diamond buckles and an ell of Brussels lace,' rejoined Nell. 'Why, even young Pepys thought twice and then three times and then actually parted with real money to pay for a supper after the play opened last month – or at least, you told us he did. And I don't suppose *he* paid for a meal just to see you guzzling chicken and gargling wine!'

'If you think I lie with a man in exchange for a chicken and some wine you're mistaken,' Becky protested. 'I've a soft spot for poor Sam Pepys; his wife's a sweet little creature but too meek, and he can't keep his hands off a shapely shoulder or a well-rounded bum! So since Maria likes me, he feels he can have a quick squeeze whenever I visit them, and it takes the heat out of him for a while.'

'You're a hussy,' Nell said. 'Anyway, you've been lucky so far; not getting with child, I mean. But I'm not taking chances! Come on, we'd better run or we'll not get decent seats. And I want to buy some oranges, just for the sake of being the purchaser instead of the seller. Another new experience you see, Beck!'

'We needn't hurry too much,' Becky said, looking a little self-conscious. 'To tell you the truth, Sam and Maria are going to the play too, and Sam will save seats for us if he can.'

'Oh! Well, as long as he doesn't start squeezing me...'

'He wouldn't. Leastways, not with his wife there. They say this is to be a grand performance, with new scenery and costumes. I'm looking forward to seeing Mrs Betterton act – she is supposed to be so marvellous – and to see the King's latest woman.'

'What, has he got another, besides Barbara Palmer?' Nell said a trifle breathlessly, as they hurried along in the clear April sunshine. 'Women seem to dote on him, don't they? Yet he's nowhere near as good looking as Rochester, or Buckhurst, or even Charles Hart!'

'His thoughts are with La Belle Stewart, but she will not be his,' Becky answered. 'He'll get her in the end though, I've no doubt. And in the meantime, he's slept with so many actresses, and fruit-women, and the like...'

'The only look he ever gives me is that

fond, indulgent glance a father might bestow on a delightful child,' Nell said gloomily. 'I'm sure he thinks of me, if he thinks of me at all that is, as the child Gwyn, one of my players.'

'Well, if you're determined to keep your virginity, it's as well the King doesn't fancy you,' Becky said practically. 'It might be difficult to say no, to the King.'

'Frances Stewart manages it,' Nell pointed out. 'Oh, this must be the Opera House.'

They pushed their way through the crowded front lobby and entered the theatre, Nell glancing around her with a mixture of curiosity and contempt, for she thought that nothing could exceed the grandeur and delight of *The* Theatre, where she was one of the King's players.

The house was actually a little larger than her own theatre. Tall wax candles stood either side of the stage, many still unlit since the play had not started. The audience were slowly filling up the benches, calling to one another and gossiping whilst they waited for the royal box to be filled.

'There are the Pepys,' Becky hissed. 'Sam's kept two places free beside him.

Let's go over.'

The two girls made their way across the auditorium, greeting friends and exchanging pleasantries with men who recognised them from the stage at the King's. Mr and Mrs Pepys were flatteringly pleased to see them, Maria's thin little face lighting up as they seated themselves near her.

'The King and the Duke are here,' Samuel Pepys remarked as he sat himself down again after making his bow. 'They came into their box as you joined us, but have left again, probably to escort the ladies. I am sure Lady Castlemaine means to be present.'

'Yes, I must remember to call her Lady Castlemaine and not merely Barbara Palmer,' Nell said reflectively. 'I prefer La Belle Stewart myself, but so does the King, evidently. I wonder what title she will win when she falls?'

'Lady Castlemaine is the most beautiful woman in England,' Pepys said stiffly. 'I find the Stewart woman insipid. Why, Castlemaine must be fair, to have gained the King's love.'

'She and thirty or forty others,' Nell said,

and laughed to see Pepys's quick, guilty glance around to make sure they'd not been overhead. 'For shame, Mr Pepys, the King himself knows he is nicknamed "Old Rowley", and thinks no shame to it.'

'Why? I've never thought to ask,' Maria said in a half-whisper.

'I thought all London knew,' Nell said. 'Old Rowley is the chief stallion in the royal stud; mad for the mares, he is.'

The inference being obvious, Mrs Pepys smiled timidly and lapsed into silence, turning in her seat every now and then to watch for the appearance of the King's party in the royal box.

They arrived at last, the King with Castlemaine on his arm and Frances Stewart accompanying the Queen, the Duke of York with a heavy, sullen looking female with an undershot jaw like a bulldog's, and three or four young men of the court.

Nell looked at them with interest, tempered by knowledge. The King was a frequent visitor to Drury Lane. And then the curtain rose, the play began, and Nell's attention was focussed on the stage. The acting was good, the singing better, the costumes and scenery, perhaps, best of all. For Becky and Nell the theatre was in their blood and whilst players were on stage, everything else took second place.

When it was over they wandered, still with minds alight from the colour and action of the play, home along the bustling early evening streets.

Nell broke the comfortable silence. 'It is a good few weeks since *we've* had such an audience, Beck! Can it be that the Duke's players are overtaking us in popularity?'

Becky frowned. 'Good God, Nellie, haven't you heard the plague has struck in some of the poorer districts of the city? There was a full house today because this play was lauded to the skies, but I heard Mr Killigrew talking to Mr Hart the other day, and he said if audiences got much thinner, we would have to close the theatre down for the summer, at least.'

'Close it down? Oh, he'd sooner die,' Nell said with conviction. 'I don't think it will come to *that*, Becky!'

'The King has said the theatres are to shut. But no-one tells us how we are to live, with our work gone.'

Nell spoke sadly, sitting on the empty stage, looking out onto the empty auditorium, with the Marshall sisters beside her.

'We shall go home, to Maidstone,' Ann Marshall said decisively. 'There is nothing for us here except a better chance of catching the plague, for there are several doors marked in the Lane already. What about you, Nellie?'

'My sister has gone. She's a lover who is an equerry at court, and they went down to Hampton Court and later, to Salisbury. But I've no lover, and no relatives in the country. Ma says she'll stay in London so I suppose I'll do the same. Perhaps I could get my old job back, at Madam Ross's house.'

'They ought to close the brothels,' Becky grumbled. 'What better way to spread plague than to sleep hip to hip with it?'

Nell shrugged. 'It is comforting, sometimes, to be with someone else,' she said. 'Where will the other players go?'

'Some will go to relatives in the country, others will stay, I suppose,' Ann said. 'You'd best talk to the others, Nell, and see if anyone can take you in. Our father is only a parson, and he's daughters enough of his own, or we would take you.'

After she had helped the Marshall sisters to pack, Nell set off to her lodgings. Her landlady, talkative Mrs Hollingtoft, asked, 'Will you leave London, dearie? Your old Ma swears she never will! She came here this afternoon for a gossip, and I told her the theatres were closing. "Then I'll not leave," she says, bold as you please. "The more women who go, the greater chances of those who remain."'

If she wants men to lie with, she ought to go down to Portsmouth,' Nell snapped uncharitably. 'The fleet would suffice for her, I'm sure.'

'And the sea-air may keep the plague at bay,' Mrs Hollingcroft agreed. 'What a good idea, Nellie.'

And Nell, who had not meant the remark kindly, had the grace to feel ashamed.

She did not go to visit her mother, however. Sitting in the overcrowded, pleasant little room she made herself a meal of cold meat and bread, poured some ale to drink and brooded over her future. What *was* she to do? She had savings, sure enough, but

they would not keep her for months, perhaps until the winter, when the cold would
chase the plague away, and the King would
reopen the theatres. If she had taken a lover
she could have gone with him, into the
country, or with the court. But it was no
use regretting that; she had had chances
enough, and she had taken none of them.

She was still brooding, the meat and bread
untouched before her, when there was a tap
on the door and Charles Hart came in,
saying, 'Feeling blue, Nell? A fine thing,
isn't it, when we lose our jobs through no
fault of our own? But the King has sent
some money for each of us. I've brought you
yours.'

Nell felt her courage rise once more.
'Thank you,' she said, holding out her hand
for the purse he offered her. 'Would you like
some supper, Mr Hart? I've plenty of meat
and bread, and ale of course.'

'Aye, I could do with a bite,' Hart said. He
sat down on a small velvet chair and looked
round him approvingly. 'This is very charming, Nell!'

'It is nice, isn't it?' Nell looked lovingly
around her parlour. 'But how long can I

keep it, without a job? I doubt Madam Ross will have me back as a servant, and I don't intend going back as a whore!'

'Still determined to reach the top?' Hart asked, cutting himself a slice of meat. 'Well, I'm off today. I shall make my way to Tunbridge Wells, for I've a sister who runs a farm near there. If I help with her stock, she'll feed me. And I reckon I shall stand less chance of catching the plague down there, than here in this stinking heat.'

'Yes, it is hot. But hot or not, it is where I shall have to stay. My Ma won't move, for a start, and I've nowhere to go anyway, for a finish!'

'Well, how about coming with me?' Hart said. 'It will mean hard work, mind, but I reckon it's healthier out of doors than in, in this weather. I'd welcome your company, Nell, if you'd like to come to the Wells. My sister'll be glad to give you a bed and food in return for help on the farm.'

'And what do I pay *you* for the privilege, Mr Hart?' Nell said cheekily. 'You know what you've told me, I am not to fall for a baby until I'm famous!'

He smiled back at her. 'What can I say,

except that it is still true? It sounds insulting to say that pretty though you are, you're not for me! You're a child still, Nellie. And besides, my sister would never stand for me taking a mistress into her house. I'll explain that you're a principal actress of the future, and that I want to keep you from temptation. Will you come?'

'As soon as I've seen my Ma and told her where I'm bound,' she said briskly. 'You stay here, and put a few things into a bag for me. You'll know better than I what to pack for staying on a farm. I shall be back presently.'

Rather to Nell's surprise, her mother raised not the slightest demur at her daughter's defection, if such it could be called. 'Me? *I'll* be all right,' she said. 'I'll work on the stall as usual, and get better money too, because there won't be many willing to work down here, with the plague an' all. And Madam Ross says I can help out there, in the evenings.'

'Try to keep off the drink,' Nell said, without much hope. She pressed the purse Hart had given her into her mother's hand. 'Here's a bit of money for you, which the King gave all his players. I shan't need it where I'm going.'

Mrs Gwyn's thanks were perfunctory, but she pocketed the money speedily and bade Nell goodbye with every appearance of complacency.

Nell then broke the news to Mrs Hollingtoft, who promised to keep the rooms empty until her return, and then rejoined Hart in her parlour.

'I've got my savings in a bag round my waist,' she told him, dimpling. 'And you've packed me a few clothes, haven't you? Then shall we leave?'

He picked up her bag and handed it to her, grinning. 'Travelling light, eh? Well done, Nellie. And with luck we shall be with my sister Mattie in a day or so.'

'The plague is killing half London,' Nell said, scanning the news-sheet which Hart had brought back to the farm after a trip to Tunbridge Wells market. 'I hope Ma is still well.'

Martha Hart sniffed. 'If, as you say, she's pickled in brandy, likely she's safer than most. Any news of the war?'

'The Dutch fleet were beaten by our lads,

and though they still threaten, have not again attempted to engage our fleet. But our fleet took quite a battering. And now the plague has hit the sailors,' Nell told her. 'Bad news on every front, is there not? Yet it's hard to believe things are so bad when here all is sunshine and gentle breezes, with your good cooking to eat!'

Martha sniffed again, but Nell could see she was pleased. 'You're putting flesh on, I can see that,' she admitted grudgingly. 'I daresay my cooking's got something to do with it. I only hope my brother keeps his hands off you.'

'He's managed to do so without any great effort so far,' Nell said regretfully. She told herself that she'd no desire for his embraces but it was curiously humiliating that he showed not the slightest desire to annoy her with his attentions! His friendship remained brotherly although there were no other females on the farm or nearby and he continued to hear her read, to coach her acting, and to demonstrate to her how to charm a sophisticated and difficult audience.

'Well, whilst he's under my roof I'll stand no nonsense,' Martha said briskly. 'Finished with that paper yet? If so, you can give me a hand with the supper. Did you bake those milk loaves like I taught you?'

'I think so. I stood them on the dresser,' Nell said. 'Are they all right, Martha? They smell *so* good, but I suppose that's nothing to go by.'

Martha picked a loaf up, tapped it, rubbed her fingers across the shiny crust, and finally broke a small piece off and put it in her mouth. 'Not bad, not bad,' she said finally, swallowing. 'We'll make a cook of you yet!'

The weeks and then the months passed. Nell was growing up. Her slight figure began to grow curves, her movements became more graceful, even her voice changed from the shrill, high notes of a child to a sweeter tone.

Charles Hart admired the change, but seemed to see it only as adding to her charms as an actress. 'It will stand you in good stead, if the theatres ever open again that is,' he said gloomily, for there was no sign that they might do so.

And then, one rainy August day, when Nell was standing in the stackyard with a sack over her head, trying to bring a smouldering bonfire to blaze in spite of the weather, a messenger came. He wanted Hart so Nell, in the working dress which left her ankles bare and with the sack still covering her hair, waited until he had left and then ran across the yard and into the farm kitchen.

As soon as she entered, Hart crossed the room in a couple of strides and picked her up in his arms, swinging her round until the sack flew off and her plume of coppery hair flew out behind her, whirling about her like a living flame.

'It's come, it's come,' he shouted exultantly, setting her on her feet again. 'Killigrew wants us back! There is a new play, and the theatres are to open, and though they do not think crowds should congregate until Christmas, when the weather should be cold enough to kill any lingering plague smells, we are to return to London on half pay until then. We must open the theatre, and rehearse, and prepare!'

Nell flung her arms round his waist and hugged him hard, her face alight with excitement. 'Oh, to be on the stage again,' she breathed. 'To hear an audience laugh, and cheer, and clap!'

'Aye,' Hart said contentedly. 'And to smell the smoke from the pipes, and the burning of wax and tallow, and the oranges from the pit. To feel the paint on your face, even!'

'A couple of great fools you be,' grumbled a voice behind them. 'Such talk! Can you find nothing better to rejoice over than a noisy crowd and their nasty smells?'

'Martha, you can't begin to know how we've missed the theatre,' Hart said, turning to face his sister. His arm round Nell, he suddenly became aware of how they must look. A tall man in a patched smock, his hair slicked to his head with rain, dust clinging to him, as did the diminutive girl, long red hair speckled with corn bits from the sack, her gown rucked up at the waist to leave her feet free. A regular yokel and his peasant wench, he thought.

'Who would ever know we were King's players,' he said, grinning at his sister. 'A good thing our audience can't see us now, eh, Nellie? They would not give us even half a cheer!'

Martha looked at them. Her handsome,

intelligent brother who had done so well for himself and the bedraggled little guttersnipe who had turned into such a beautiful and hard-working young woman. And now they would go and leave her lonesome. Before they came she had been content enough with her life, not missing company she had never known. But she had no words to express her feelings. Instead, she said gruffly, 'You don't look so bad to me, either of ye,' and then turned and stumped back into the dairy.

Nell let go of Hart's arm and followed Miss Martha Hart's broad back into the dairy. She said timidly, 'I'll never forget all you've done for me, Martha. You've taught me to enjoy the country, you've shown me how to cook, and clean, and make and mend. And I've learned many another thing, as well. May I come back and see you, some time?'

'Aye, and welcome,' Martha said gruffly. 'Come wi' Charlie, or by yourself. Now be off with you both, and pack up your bits of things. *Someone* must do some work this day!'

# Four

Nell lay in the small truckle bed in her mother's tiny, cramped lodging room, and wondered wearily how she could possibly be so tired, yet still not be able to sleep. She and Hart had returned to London post haste, to find their old companions gathering, old rooms being reopened, and old plays being re-read.

But for Nell, there had been no homecoming. Mrs Hollingtoft's house, closed and shuttered, gave few clues, but 'they died of the plague,' a neighbour said darkly. 'It is owned by a nephew now, but heaven knows, missus, if you'll ever see your stuff again. And what loss? 'Tis said she died in your room.'

So Nell had been glad enough to rejoin her mother, who seemed to have thrived despite the sickness and despair all about her. Perhaps Martha was right, and brandy can keep off the plague, Nell thought, regarding the filth and muddle of the small room. She had set to with a will and cleaned it up to the best of her ability, though without much hope of it remaining neat, for as drink became more important to her, Mrs Gwyn's interest in housework, never strong, dwindled further.

Rose was back, still in the keeping of a gentleman friend, but they had not met. And now, back in London with the theatre not a stone's throw away, she could not sleep! It seemed hot in bed, and airless. She longed for the buffeting wind which she had cursed at the farm. She remembered her narrow pallet in the little, whitewashed room under the eaves, and suppressed a pang of longing. Of *course* she would sooner be in London than there! She was a cockney, born and bred, and more at home in London than anywhere else on earth.

She turned on her back and wondered whether she should creep out of bed and open the window. But it led directly onto the street, and she didn't fancy some stray vagabond taking advantage of such seeming carelessness, so that he hooked his leg over the sill and came in to find what he could steal. In the bed against the wall, her mother stirred and muttered. Nell sat up and reached cautiously for her petticoat. She would slip that on, and get herself a cool drink; then perhaps she would be able to sleep.

Yawning, she moved across the room, opened the door, and went into the kitchen which the lodgers shared. As she did so, she glanced towards the window. Over the rooftops, she could see a pink glow in the sky. Oh, so dawn was near, was it? Then she might as well dress, and walk down to the market. Her mother would soon be off to work in any case.

As she poured herself ale, she sniffed. A faint, acrid smell seemed to enter the house as the sky grew lighter. Of course, she had forgotten; houses did catch fire sometimes, and then the timber frame and the thatched roofs went up like tinder. Not that many houses in London were thatched, but most were heavily tarred, to keep out the weather. In the other room she heard her mother stir, and poured another mug of ale. They might as well get up together, for Mrs Gwyn had no desire to lose her job in the market by being late, and had trained herself to wake when the morning light fell upon her face.

'Ma, I'm awake, so I shall come to the market with you,' she said re-entering their rooms and giving her mother's recumbent form a dig.

Mrs Gwyn muttered, then sat up slowly, saying in a voice still thick with sleep, 'I had forgot you were back, Nellie! Coming to the market, are you? I remember when you came each morning, to buy oranges for your basket. Ah, it seems a long time ago now. A long, long time.'

Nell fancied she heard a wistful note in her mother's voice, and thought, don't say she's going to get a fancy for my company, for she had not the smallest intention of remaining with Mrs Gwyn once she had found a decent lodging for herself. Hurriedly, therefore, she said, 'I couldn't sleep, for I was too hot. And there's a fire near at hand, I reckon, for I can smell burning.'

Mrs Gwyn heaved herself out of bed and snorted contemptuously. 'During the plague they burned bonfires outside the front doors because they thought it would kill the disease. Now I suppose they're burning the plague houses themselves.'

'I hope not!' Nell said, alarmed. 'My furniture is still at Mrs Hollingtoft's, and my turkey carpet, and a stack of clothes which I wore on the stage.'

'You don't want that stuff. She died on that turkey carpet, I daresay,' Mrs Gwyn said. She had slept fully clothed despite the heat but now she reached for her shawl and pulled it round her shoulders. 'And anyway, the fire can't be at Hollingtoft's, or we'd see it as well as smell it. And now, gal, we'd best be...' she stopped in mid-sentence, staring at her daughter with rising indignation. 'Nell, what be you about, rousing me? 'Tis Sunday, and not even that old rascal fat Fred would expect me to work on a Sunday!'

'Oh, no,' moaned Nell. With the realisation that it was, in fact, Sunday, came an increasing need to be up and doing, for they would not rehearse today. Mrs Gwyn, casting off her shawl, did not waste time on further talk, but rolled, grunting, back into bed and pulled the blankets up round her ears. Nell looked at her own bed and sighed. She could not go back to sleep, but what would be the point of getting up? Unless, of course, she strolled down to Charles Hart's lodgings, or visited her friend, Betty Ball, for Betty was also back at her old lodgings and it was not too far away.

Nell glanced towards the window again. The day was bright now, and she thought that the pink glow, which was still in evidence had not been the dawn, but a fire.

'I'll walk down and take a look at the fire,' she told her mother's hunched form. 'I shan't be long, and if I can find a baker open, I'll buy us a fresh loaf, and some currant buns.'

A grumbling groan from the bed made her smile, but she slipped a cloak over her shoulders and set off, glad, as soon as she opened the front door, to be out in the freshness of the morning, away from the frowsty room which still smelled, despite her cleaning, of stale drink, stale food, and stale air.

It was a windy day, the gale roaring amongst the rooftops and pulling at her cloak. No-one was about at first, and she walked along swiftly until she came to Betty's lodgings. Betty was still abed, the house bolted and quiet, so Nell decided to call on Hart and see how he was faring. He was living in a handsome house in Queen Street, and Nell quite expected to find him, if not actually in bed, at least still breakfasting. But when she turned the corner into his street the first thing which met her eyes was his tall figure, coming down his front steps, his coat half-buttoned, his head bare.

'Charlie!' She shouted into the wind, but a gust carried her voice away and she was forced to halloo with an actor's clarity, running down the street towards him, before he turned and saw her.

'Good morning, Nell,' he said jovially. 'And where might you be going? Or have you been carried here by the wind, against your will? It is strong enough to lift a little thing like you!'

'Anchor me down, then,' Nell said, clutching at his coat. She smiled up at him, reflecting that in the country he had seemed like a blissful breath of Drury Lane and London, and here in Queen Street he brought back the happiest times on the farm.

He laughed with her, but said, 'I'm going to buy some breakfast for the prettiest lass in the company. She desires sugar buns.'

Nell felt her heart miss a beat. She said, 'Sugar buns! Does she lodge in your house, then?'

He laughed again, saying, 'Don't pretend innocence, Nell! You must have seen I was taken by her, at rehearsals! Ah, she's the loveliest woman, and bids fair to become a good actress, too.'

Nell, by a dint of furious thinking, conjured up a picture of a golden haired, langorous creature, generously built, who had been making eyes at Hart all through rehearsal the previous day.

'Barbary Lacy, do you mean?' she said incredulously. 'But she isn't an actress, Charlie. She's just stage-struck, and wants men.'

'No, no,' he protested. 'She wants to be an actress. She stayed with me last night – what a woman she is, in bed – and tomorrow I shall put her forward, so that Killigrew notices her. She has great beauty, you know.'

'Takes more than that to make an actress,' Nell muttered. 'I've been on the stage since I was thirteen, and I'm still learning.'

'Aye, and learning well,' he responded, a little absently. 'What are those people doing?'

'Moving house, most likely,' Nell said, watching a cart laden with all manner of household goods draw up outside a substantial house. The driver of the cart, an elderly man, got down and began to bang on the door. As soon as it opened he began a garbled explanation, not much helped by the fact that he was toothless.

'Oh, he's fled from a fire,' Nell said, suddenly getting the gist of the elderly man's lament. 'Of course, Charlie, I saw the flames in the sky when I first woke. Do come and see it with me! We could go down to the Thames and get a boat if it's too far to walk.'

But Hart shook his head. 'Got to take sugar buns back to my sugar darling,' he said in an infatuated tone which Nell thought absurd for a man of his years. But she knew better than to say so, for even if Hart was not interested in her as a woman, he could still ruin her career as an actress if he so chose.

'All right, I'll go alone,' Nell was beginning, when her companion grasped her arm. 'Am I seeing things? Look there, Nellie!'

They were on rising ground and could see, far off, a church steeple being consumed by flames; roaring, blazing, and suddenly, falling.

'Barbary will have to wait for her sugar cakes,' Hart said, his voice rising with excitement. 'Come on lass, we mustn't miss this!'

And hand in hand they ran down Fleet Street, towards the smell of smoke.

The fire of London raged for a week and for all that time, Nell and Hart stayed in the city, doing their utmost to help quench the flames by any means, for the east wind was driving the inferno towards Drury Lane, and the theatre. At first no effort was made to stop the fire from consuming house after house, for everyone thought only of themselves and their own property. But then the King and the Duke of York came on the scene and began, not only to order the pulling down of houses in the path of the fire, but to give aid themselves in the carrying out of their orders.

So when the King noticed Hart – 'one of my players working to save his theatre, eh?' – it was natural for he and Nell to join the courtiers who worked with their sovereign to try to finish the fire before it finished London. Sweating, grimy and totally exhausted, they formed chains to pass buckets of water, strove to cut down charred timbers, scattered burning thatch, and worked like demons until they fell into exhausted sleep at the end of each day, in some church or public building which the fire had not yet touched.

On the first day, Nell had changed her petticoats for shirt and breeches, and at first the courtiers chaffed her, but soon everyone was too tired and anxious for much chatter – the situation was too desperate. Rochester, Sedley, Buckingham, Clarges and Buckhurst, men whom Nell had often seen in her audience when she trod the boards at the King's House, now worked beside her, faces blackened, silks and satins in rags, fighting to save London.

On the third day, when Nell and Hart were snatching a moment to sit down and rest their aching backs and drink some milk, Buckhurst flung himself down beside them. 'I'll have a drink when you've done,' he said wearily, and Nell, without comment, passed the bottle over. He took a long pull and grimaced, wiping his mouth on his sleeve and smearing his face with black. 'Milk! Good God, I thought you would be drinking something a bit more interesting than that!' He exclaimed. He grinned across at Nell. 'I've watched you with admiration on the stage, and now that I know you only need milk to keep you so lively, my admiration is doubled! If I ask you to sup with me, when this is over, will you condescend to drink wine, my pretty? Or will I have to send to the country for milk?'

Answering in the same vein, Nell said, 'Usually, sir, I only bath in milk. But since I am prevented from doing that, I determined to drink the stuff so that it doesn't go to waste. And as to supping with you, that will depend first, on whether there is a theatre left for me to grace, and second, whether you've a home left, with a table fit to spread a supper on!'

'Very true,' he said. A distant halloo was

followed by a tremendous roar and crash, gradually fading into silence.

'Ah, that will be the army, blowing up houses which are in the fire's path,' Buckhurst informed them. 'It was the King's idea, and if it halts the flames, then it is a good one. I only hope *my* house isn't blown sky-high, though.'

He sketched a bow to them, gave Nell one last, twinkling glance and was gone.

'Charles Sackville, Lord Buckhurst,' Hart said idly. 'The wildest of a wild bunch, but he works like a man, Nell. And he's a clever fellow, by all accounts. He seemed to admire you, my child.'

'Ho, very likely,' Nell scoffed. 'In filthy breeches, with my shirt torn and my hair thick with ash! I'm sure he thinks me a disgrace to the profession.'

Hart chuckled. 'Which profession?' he asked. 'But he'd notice your pretty figure if you were dressed in a sack, that one would. He's a devil for the women. It would be a fine thing for you, if he took you up.'

'Oh, I suppose he doesn't beget babies?' Nell said sarcastically, getting to her feet. 'I've got no time for men, Charlie, be they never so rich or handsome. Come on, to work again.'

And they toiled on, forgetting everything but the task in hand.

And then, on the fifth day, when it really seemed that their work would soon be finished, Nell ventured into a pastry cook's little house, next door to a big lodging house which would presently be blown up, for the surer stopping of the fire. She had heard the cry of some child or animal, and called to Hart, 'Charlie! I'm going in. There's something alive inside.'

Her search of the house proved abortive, and she was about to leave again when she heard a faint cry from beneath her feet and thought, someone is down in the cellar. She knew that people had buried their wine and other valuables beneath their houses and thought it possible that a child trying to rob had been caught below. It was the work of a moment to find the cellar door. She opened it without difficulty, peering into the darkness. 'Hey, is anybody down there?' She called, and was rewarded by a faint scraping in one corner of the pitch-black cellar. She began to descend the stairs, one hand held out before her so that she would not walk straight into an obstacle. Behind her, she heard someone else beginning to descend the steps, and then something brushed her ankles and in the light from the doorway she saw a skinny kitten, every hair on end, rush up the remaining stairs and into the light-ened room above.

'Come out, Nell, it is dangerous...' A voice began, and then the words were cut off by the most appalling, earth-shattering roar and the sound of falling masonry.

Nell was hurled across the cellar by the blast and lay against the far wall, feeling as though her skin had been stripped from her bones. The light had gone completely and she was in total darkness, the only sound came as more masonry fell, and plaster trickled, and something warm and sticky ran from her hair down her cheek.

As the sounds gradually faded into silence, she sat up, gingerly feeling her face. 'Char-lie? Are you there? Are you alive?' She said in a small voice into the darkness.

A hand scraped along the floor somewhere not far off and Hart's voice, husky, cracked, and almost unrecognisable, said shakily,

'Nell? I'm all right. You?'

She gave a sob of relief. 'I'm a bit shaken, Charlie, and there's blood on my face. But I'm alive! Wait a bit, I'm near the wall. I'll see if I can get over to you.'

She tried to move but bumped almost immediately into a heavy timber beam, and gave a gasp as she felt the beam vibrate.

'Don't worry, I know where you are now,' Hart said. 'I *was* under that beam, but I was just pulling myself out when you bumped into it. If I work my way along...'

He suited action to words and Nell suddenly felt his arms go round her in a hard hug.

'Don't worry, we'll soon be out of here, they'll miss us quickly enough,' he muttered into her hair. 'There, you cry if you want to, poor child.'

Afterwards, Nell thought wonderingly that some madness must have seized her. She was sitting quiet in his arms one moment, and the next they were locked in a tight embrace, kissing passionately, and she made no protest when his hands began to explore her body, nor when he wrenched open her shirt to fondle her breasts.

He was half on top of her then, breathing quickly, but she felt him hesitate. A part of her mind told her that if she wanted to stop him, now was the moment, but instead she began to wriggle out of her borrowed breeches, wanting him so badly that she could scarcely bear the short delay.

And then he was on her, gentle despite his urgency, caressing her and speaking gentle love-words, until their bodies fused in mutual need, mutual hunger.

She cried out then, saying, 'Charlie, oh Charlie,' and pressed herself closer to him, not heeding the pain of his entry but rejoicing in the fierce flood of pleasure which followed. She heard him say wonderingly, even as he drove into her, 'A virgin! My dear child, you're a virgin!' but scarcely realised the significance of his surprise.

'Yours now, Charlie,' she said as they lay quiet at last, hearts hammering, his lips soft against her neck. 'No more need for Barbary Lacy now, and no more need for me to feel jealous of her.'

He was silent, holding her close.

And strangely, despite their danger and her happiness, she fell asleep in his arms, as happily and securely as though she was in her own bed.

She woke when he called her by name, and shook her shoulder gently. 'Wake up, Nellie,' he said, and she could hear laughter in his voice. 'Put your breeches on, girl! I've been trying to get them on for you, but I'm not much of a hand at it, in pitch dark.'

'No, you're probably better at getting them off,' Nell agreed, sitting up and struggling into her clothes again. 'But why, Charlie? Are we to be rescued? Is that why I must dress?'

He was unable to resist asking, 'Why don't you want to dress? Do you want to make love again?' and was flattered and delighted by her shy, 'I *would* like to make love again!'

'We will; but later, love,' he said, stroking her cheek. 'They've been trying to break the door down, but now they're removing masonry from around the frame, and we shall soon be free.'

Even as he spoke they saw light, across the cellar, and then a flood of it as someone broke right through to them. The hole was temporarily filled as a figure squeezed through and stood on the topmost step, and then a man's voice said sharply, 'Nellie? Are you all right?'

Light flowered as a candle was handed through the aperture and he held it up, flooding the cellar with light and illumining his own face. 'Come out carefully,' he warned, 'or the main beam may collapse and kill us all.'

And it was Charles Hart.

Nell spun round with a gasp, to face the man who had been making love to her a few minutes earlier. Despite a coating of dust and plaster, she had no difficulty in recognising Charles Sackville, Lord Buckhurst.

# Five

'And this is to be your big chance, Nell. You will take the part of Lady Wealthy, in *The English Monsieur*. It is a comic part, and one which I know you will do well. Are you pleased.'

'Yes, I'm thrilled,' Nell said, giving Hart the benefit of her widest smile. 'I wonder who will play opposite me?'

Hart grinned goodnaturedly. 'Who else but myself? But Nell, you've waited so long for a really good part which will show you at your comic best. Why aren't you over the moon? You've been quiet and withdrawn ever since we started rehearsals.'

Nell shrugged, saying casually, 'Well, *The Maid's Tragedy* wasn't the sort of play I thought suited me, though I did my best in it. I was beginning to think laughter had gone out of fashion, what with the plague, and the Great Fire.'

'We need laughter more than anything else, to make us forget our troubles,' Hart said. They were standing on the stage with the other members of the cast and he turned to Barbary Lacy, waiting in the wings. 'Barbary, fetch my copy of the play. And be quick!'

He moved away, and 'Not even a please,' Nell murmured to Becky, who stood near her. 'To be that man's mistress is not all roses, one can see that!'

'No, better take a gallant from the court, if you've a mind to fall,' Becky agreed. 'They've more money, and more respect for our calling. Oh, look, Buckhurst's in the auditorium again. He loves rehearsals as much as performances, if you ask me.'

Nell felt the blood rush to her face, but she merely said, 'He loves the theatre as we all do. And he's not averse to actresses, either.'

'Yes. He's after someone,' agreed Becky. 'He doesn't say much, but he's out front, night after night.'

'If you ladies have finished your private discussion.' Hart said sarcastically, 'we will commence our rehearsal.'

Becky waited until he had his back to them again and then stuck her tongue out. 'He thinks he's so marvellous,' she muttered. 'He's only a player, like us.'

'Are you nervous, Nellie?'

Nell finished painting a cupid's bow on her upper lip and swung round from the mirror. She put her hand to her breast, fluttered her eyelashes, and said, in the well-bred drawl which she assumed for the character of Lady Wealthy, 'Indeed to God I am, good sir! Yet I know it is a fair part, and I shall do fairly well in it.'

Hart, swinging into his character with equal ease, said, with a lisp, 'Certes, no need for nerves, me pretty! I'll see thee right, and if thou forgetst thy lines why, pull a pretty face, and the King will forgive thee all!'

'The King! He is here already then?'

'Of course. With Castlemaine beside him and his latest mare, the little Stewart.'

'She isn't his mare,' objected Nell. 'That is well-known, Charlie! Oh, I'll not deny that he wants her, but you know full well she holds back.'

'She's the only one, then,' Hart said. 'Do *you* find him attractive, Nell? Apart from his high position, I mean.'

'He's not handsome, yet I do find him attractive. Not that he ever looks at me,' Nell said fairly.

'Of course not,' Hart said with unconscious cruelty. 'You're only a child, Nellie. But growing up fast, I will admit.'

She smiled at him, patting powder onto her arms to hide the dusting of golden freckles which the sun had painted during her sojourn at the Hart farm. 'I am,' she agreed, 'And now let us go and view our audience from behind the curtain.'

They went onto the stage together, murmuring greetings to other players who stood waiting in tense little groups. Betty Ball, playing a serving wench, whispered 'Good luck, Nellie,' as the couple passed.

'It's a good audience,' Hart murmured, his eye to a crack in the curtains. 'See the King, Nellie? And Castle-maine? And La Belle Stewart?'

'Yes, and she's twice as pretty as Barbara,' said Nell. 'Who's that thin, pale girl with the Duke of York? Barbara is putting on weight and looks sulky.'

'The girl with James is Arabella Churchill,' Hart said. 'Did you hear how James came to take her for his mistress?'

Nell stood back. 'Let's take up our positions for the first act, as they are all here,' she suggested. 'And you can tell me then.'

They stood in the wing, waiting, whilst Hart murmured the story of how Miss Churchill, being but a poor horse-woman, was thrown on the hunting field, and James, hurrying to pick her up, had seen that though her face might be plain, her body was so perfectly formed as to be almost unbelievable.

'She was virtuous, they say, but is so no longer,' Hart whispered mischievously. 'The Duke is even more lecherous than the King, if that's possible. But he likes plain women, for some reason, though he insists on beautiful figures.'

'He's a very plain man, perhaps that's why,' Nell suggested. 'The King, whatever one may call him, is far from plain. Ugly, interesting, but never plain and dull. Poor Dismal Jimmy; I hope he and his Arabella will be very happy.'

They were still chuckling when the curtain began to move with a heavy rustle. For a moment she hung back, small, nervous, wide-eyed, and then she gathered herself together and before Hart's eyes became Lady Wealthy whose beauty, wit and poise were legendary. She put up a hand to tuck an errant curl into place, and swept past him onto the stage, her first lines already on her lips. From where he stood he could almost feel the audience's pleasure and interest rise to meet her. He smiled. She would be all right!

'Nellie, there's a gentleman wants to see you!'

Nellie, struggling out of her pink and white gown, cursed briefly, and grinned at the girl who had poked her head into the room. She dropped the gown on the floor and tied a wrap round her. Glancing quickly in the mirror, she saw that her face and hair would pass muster, though she had yet to clean her makeup off the one and brush the other.

'Let him come in,' she said resignedly, adding, as the girl disappeared, 'Who is it, anyway?'

'It is I, Sackville,' a voice said, and Lord Buckhurst came round the door. Nell felt her face go hot and turned at once to the glass, digging her fingers into the pot of grease to remove her makeup.

'What do you want?' she said coldly. 'I didn't know it was you, I thought it was young Killigrew.'

'I know. If you'd known it was me you would not have let me in. Nellie, what else must I say to show you I'm sorry? Sorry about what happened in the cellar in Newgate Street, I mean.'

Nellie plastered on the grease, glancing at him through the mirror with resentful eyes. Speaking carefully, so that she did not invade her mouth with the stuff, she said, 'You can say nothing. And I want nothing to do with you. Go at once, do you hear me?'

But he shut the door and advanced into the room, until he was standing close behind her, his hands on her shoulders. She stiffened but did not draw away, continuing to clean her skin as though she were alone.

'Nellie, I love you,' he pleaded. 'I've admitted it was a rotten trick, to let you believe I was Charles Hart, and then to make love to you. But I didn't know you were a virgin, I thought you'd had dozens of men and I would be just another. You think I cannot know how you feel, but I do! You feel humiliated and ashamed, and you want to forget that wrong man or not, you enjoyed it. But what of *me*? I meant no harm, yet by loving you I've earned your hatred.'

Nell wiped off the last of her paint and, still ignoring him, went over to the water bowl and dunked her face in the water, shivered, and reached blindly for the towel. It was not beside her, but she felt him put it into her hands.

'I would give you *everything*,' he pleaded softly. 'My dearest little love, will you not listen to me? Am I so repulsive? Dine with me tonight, and at least give me the pleasure of watching you whilst you eat.'

'Dine where?' Nell said suspiciously. 'Anyway, I'm tired.'

'Wherever you wish,' he said at once. He hesitated, then moved towards the door. 'You will want to change out of your wrap. Shall I wait outside?'

For some reason, it touched her that this man, a hardened rake who had tricked her out of her virginity, should offer to leave the room whilst she took off her wrap and replaced it with a gown. She smiled at him, melting suddenly into friendliness.

'There's no need,' she said, and saw him brighten, his face expressing his pleasure at her decision.

She took off her wrap and dropped it onto a chair and stood before him, face free from makeup now, hair brushed clean from powder, in her nice white petticoat, looking like a good child. 'It is not right that I should punish you for my own foolishness,' she said frankly, picking up a green, trained skirt and stepping into it. 'You see, my lord, I *wanted* you to be someone else. I daresay you've guessed who, but it doesn't matter. He doesn't even consider me a woman. Pass me my bodice, would you?'

He passed it, watching as she fastened the boned creation which pushed her breasts up so that they showed, round and pink and tempting, above the frills of her chemise. 'And another thing which annoyed me,' she went on, apparently not noticing his absorption in her employment, 'Was that I should lose my virginity so ... so casually, to a man I'd not really met. I had meant to save it for ... for someone special.'

Restraining himself with the utmost difficulty from touching her, he said hoarsely, 'But I *want* to be someone special to you! I want you to come and live with me, have I not said it time after time? I am a close friend of the King's, and the Duke's too, for that matter. You shall mix with the best people, I swear it!'

'But you yourself can scarcely be numbered amongst the best people,' Nell said naughtily. 'You are a known womaniser, you are wild to a fault, you drink too much, and you are always in trouble. You danced naked through the streets last midwinter, and you have been guilty of many crimes. Once, they whispered you should have been charged with murder; only your intimacy with the King saved you. How can I ally myself to such a man?'

He grinned guiltily, acknowledging the truth of her remarks with a half-nod. 'Others are worse, Nellie. And I write pretty verse, and some good plays. I'm not bad looking, am I, and I'm young, not like some of the old rakes who haunt the theatres, searching for someone to titillate their jaded senses. Nellie, look at me!'

Nell, fully dressed now in the splendours of her green silk gown, looked. She saw a tall, well-built man in his late twenties with a sensitive, sensuous face, the eyes melting with affection for her, the mouth curled into a hopeful half smile.

She laughed at him suddenly, her eyes narrowing to slits of amusement. 'You forgot to say that you make love very competently, even upon a cellar floor,' she said, gasping with mirth and clutching her side. 'Dear God, how conceited men are!'

But he did not rise to the bait. 'Come home with me, Nell,' he urged. 'Think how much better my lovemaking would be in a soft feather bed!'

But though she laughed and took his arm, she still shook her head. 'Oh no, sir, thank you kindly. But I will certainly dine with you!'

Nell was a tremendous success in the new play, and she continued to see Lord Buckhurst constantly, though she did not become his mistress. However, she found him a pleasant and congenial companion, and as they became easy with one another, she thought that one day, when she was sure of her position in the theatre, she might easily succumb to his charms.

'But I could not leave the theatre and go and live with him,' she told Betty, as they prepared their clothes for Dryden's new play, *The Maiden Queen*, in which Nell was to play two roles, that of a mad girl and a young gallant. 'Even though he is very charming,' she added a trifle wistfully.

'But not as charming as an audience, crying with laughter when you want them to, and clapping and cheering when you swagger about the stage as a young man,' Betty said understandingly. 'Never mind, Nell, one day you'll find a man who's worth giving it all up for.'

'They say that Charles Stuart has tossed his handkerchief to Moll Davies, at the Duke's House,' Nell said. She frowned. 'I cannot understand what he sees in her, but there, tastes differ!'

Betty laughed. 'She's quite pretty, and

she's got marvellous legs,' she said cheerfully. 'No good to expect the King to appreciate character, if he can stand Castlemaine!'

'He's pursuing Frances Stewart so hotly that it's a wonder he notices anyone else,' Nell remarked. 'And it proves La Belle Stewart's virtue if he has to seek Moll's bed!'

'Miaow!' Betty said. 'Moll *is* pretty, Nell. And what of Charlie Hart? He seems to have borne Barbary's defection with good humour. She's Charles Sedley's mistress now, isn't she?'

'Yes. And there's another good reason for not moving in with Buckhurst,' Nell said, her glance darkening. 'Sedley and Buck are close friends, and I've no mind to put myself on a par with Hart's cast-off whore.'

'No. But you are considering Buck's claim to bed you, are you not?' Betty asked curiously.

Nell smiled, wrinkling her small nose. 'Wouldn't you like to know?' she chanted derisively. 'And so would Charlie Hart, no doubt! But as yet, Buck is just my very good friend.'

And so it continued. Charles Hart showed some pique when he noticed Buckhurst dancing attendance upon Nell, and threatened to have her kept in line by a chaperon, for at the Duke's House, the manager kept his leading ladies lodged within his own home, to try to protect them from would-be seducers. But Nell just pulled a face and laughed at Hart, telling him that until she packed her bags and moved in with Buckhurst, it would be no concern of his.

Furthermore, she knew that her name now meant a lot to the theatre. The court only had to hear that Nell was in a play for the theatre to be packed. The King himself always perked up when she came upon the stage, but still, to Nell's annoyance, his expression when he watched her was that of an indulgent father. James, Duke of York, newly in love with another of his wife's waiting women, chasing La Belle Stewart neck and neck with the King, and with Arabella Churchill and Lady Denham his acknowledged mistresses, still had time to stare at her speculatively and pinch her cheek.

'But I wouldn't want Dismal Jimmy for a

lover, and he wouldn't want me,' Nell told Betty. 'I reckon he wouldn't demean himself to make an actress his mistress, and I won't lie down for a man just because he's a Duke. And anyway,' she added, dimpling, 'When I make love I intend to enjoy it, and not to see that long face bobbing above me, doing his duty and pretending to hate it!'

And indeed, had it not been for one small incident, Nell might never have given in to Lord Buckhurst, for heady though his admiration was, the applause and affection of the audiences was headier still.

All through a long, chilly spring, she continued to take major parts on the stage, and to see audiences helpless with mirth at her antics. And after the show there were intimate little supper parties at court, or with Buck, or a visit to a nobleman's home, or a theatrical gathering in her lodgings, with the men relaxed and easy, talking shop and enjoying themselves.

And then, chance stepped in. Nell was rehearsing a part in a comedy which she thought the best thing she had done yet. She was in boy's gear once more, and enjoying every moment of it and when the rehearsal was over she strolled, in her breeches and vivid green shirt, out of the theatre and round to her lodgings, hoping to give her landlady, Mrs Prothero, a surprise. It was a fine afternoon in early summer, and she sang a little song as she walked along, glad to be alive, to be healthy, and to be young and admired. In between verses, she bit into a sharp-sweet little apple, gnawing it hungrily, as a boy would have done.

As she turned the corner she saw Sedley and Buckhurst, arm in arm, strolling towards her, and wondered whether they would recognise her, and make an outcry. But though both men had an eye for a pretty girl, they had no interest whatsoever in small, red-haired urchins, chewing apples and whistling their way down the road, so she passed them by, unnoticed.

Smiling to herself at their total non-recognition, she went on her way, but to her disappointment, Mrs Prothero was out. However, she remembered that John Lacy lodged near herself and that since he was not in the present play, he had not yet seen her in costume. She ran up his front steps, rapped on the door, and walked up the stairs and into Lacy's parlour.

The room was empty, but the table was set for two. She strolled across the carpet and examined the food. A nice dinner, evidently, with cold chicken, and salad, and quite an array of side-dishes. She picked up a chicken leg and bit into it, then threw her little apple core into the empty grate. As she did so, a sound from the adjoining room caught her attention. She stopped, and glanced reflectively at the door. Of course! When she had last visited his lodgings, Lacy had shown her the small room leading off from the the main parlour. There was little furniture in there except for a day-bed and a mirror, for he used to practise his lines sitting on the day-bed and watching his own face in the mirror, she remembered now.

'And sometimes I have a nap in here,' he had gone on to explain, and she remembered that he had not been too well this past week, having caught a heavy cold. She listened again. Yes, she was almost sure it had been a little, curling snore! She would catch John snoozing and make him jump!

Taking another big bite out of the chicken leg, she crossed the room and opened the door carefully.

There was the little room, just as she remembered it. Save that instead of John Lacy, it was Charles Hart who lay on the day-bed. He was full naked. And beneath him, her hair tumbled and her petticoat rucked up to her armpits, lay Betty Ball.

They did not notice her. So engaged were they in their noisy and athletic love-play that neither so much as glanced towards the open door and Nell was able to withdraw, close the door softly behind her and run quietly down the stairs and out of the front door without disturbing them. Even when she tripped half a dozen steps from the bottom she managed to fall quietly, though shock, and the pain from a wrenched ankle, made her halt her headlong flight and brought her run down to an uneven trot.

Presently, she slowed to a walk, and told herself firmly that she was being foolish. What was so wrong, anyway? Hart was perfectly entitled to take Bet if he desired to do so, and Betty, God knows, was entirely ignorant of Nell's feelings for Charlie Hart. But the damage was done. In the space of those few shocked seconds her life had been changed. It was plain that wherever Hart looked next for a mistress, it would not be to her.

And then down the street towards her, came Buckhurst, walking fast, his coat unbuttoned, a look of fierce concentration on his face. She knew him well enough by now to know that that expression meant he was composing a poem, or a play, or some such thing, but she could not worry about disturbing his train of thought at such a moment.

'Buck!' she cried, shaking his arm. 'It is I, Nellie! Do you still want me to come and live with you?'

Startled out of his creative thought, he had barely time to stammer his desire anew before she was saying, 'Then you shall have me! I will pack my things and move into your house quicker than the cat can lick her ear!'

'But I am about to move down to Epsom for the summer,' he said, not understanding her sudden capitulation, but quick to take advantage of it.

She shrugged, her vivid little face troubled for a moment. 'I'll come too,' she decided. 'We'll have some fun, Buck!'

# Six

'I'd not have come to Epsom if I'd known you'd be here.'

'Nor I!'

Nell and Barbary Lacy stood glaring at each other across the wide living room of the house Buckhurst had hired.

'And my lord hired this house for *me*, you trollop! You and your ... your fancy man simply moved in. I shall tell Buck what I think of Sedley, and you'll soon find yourself out on your ... your ... ear.'

'Oh, just try it,' Barbary said. Then, changing her tone, 'Except that perhaps it would be as well if we were friends, Nellie. Your man's got a nasty temper, and mine has a worse. We may need one another yet.'

Nell eyed Barbary's indolent, ripe body with overt contempt. 'Need *you*? Me? Why on earth should I?'

'Because if I were to go, you might be called upon to satisfy two lusts. I have been, during my time with Sedley. Believe me, they're such good friends that they share women as well as houses! And it can be a tricky business, choosing which one to join for the night, for the other will resent your choice, that's for sure.'

Nell heaved an exaggerated sigh and walked to the window. 'All right. We'll pretend complacency, at any rate. I've no desire to lie with Sedley, you may be sure of that! He took Florry Bucknell, you know, and if she had her eye blacked once during his keeping, she had it blacked half a dozen times. But I see you've managed to remain unmarked.'

'Oh, yes. I'm too lazy to argue with him, whatever he may suggest,' Barbary said placidly. 'But you're different, Nell. You've got a sharp tongue, and you laugh a lot. Sedley wouldn't like that.'

'Sedley won't have to like it; all I want of him is to be left alone,' Nell said sharply. But she was worried. Buckhurst was proving a delightful lover most of the time, but there was no doubt that he had a nasty temper.

And Nell herself was aware that within three days of moving into his home and giving up the stage she had become bored. Furthermore, she was worried about Hart. He had been incredulous and furious when she had handed back a good, comic part which he had picked out specially for her. He had not seemed able to believe, at first, that she actually meant to leave the stage, for the summer at any rate. And when she had finally convinced him, he had gone straight to Mr Killigrew and told her he would see she never worked in London again.

'Very well, I'll apply to the Davenants. The Duke's House could do with a comedy actress,' Nell said at once, bringing a flush of such fury to Hart's face that she had incontinently fled, not wishing to find herself being smacked!

Mr Killigrew, however, was more practical. 'Charlie is only angry because he thinks highly of you,' he told her. 'He would like you for himself, you see, and cannot bear to be cast aside for Buckhurst.'

'That's not so,' Nell objected. 'He has never been rebuffed because he has never made any advances to me! If he had done so and I'd turned him down, I could under-stand it.'

'Ah, I see,' Killigrew said, his little blue eyes shrewd. 'Well, my dear, when you're tired of being a lady, come to me. Hart will soon see who's boss here, if he tries to turn away the best little comic actress I've ever worked with.'

So Nell knew that her job at least was safe, and had gone off to Epsom with only the pleased anticipation of one about to enjoy a well earned holiday.

And after only one night in the Epsom house, she had gone shopping for some lace trimming in the pleasant, countrified little town, and returned to find Barbary install-ed, and Sedley and Buckhurst off some-where.

'Once they've got you, their attitude changes,' Barbary said sadly, now. 'Hart was the same. It was all hand-holding and ogling until I fell, and then it was Barbary do this, Barbary do that, until I was little better than a slave. Why he was kinder to *you* than he was to me, and you were just another player.'

'I never was *just* a player,' Nell said

haughtily, and then, unbending, 'But now, of course, 'I'm just a kept woman and I tell you, Barbary, it's mighty boring. What do you *do* all day? I know what you do all night, of course, and mighty tired I shall get of that if it is going on every night without fail for weeks and weeks! But what about the days?'

'Well, I shop for food, and plan the meals, and tell the maids what to do,' Barbary said, ticking her tasks off on her fingers, 'And I buy cloth and go to the seamstress for fittings of new gowns. And I take the waters in the afternoons, or go for drives into the real country. And in the evenings I entertain any friends Sedley chooses to bring back.'

'Hmm,' Nell said dolefully. 'Nothing else? No parties, or fun, or visiting with friends?'

'Plenty of parties when your keeper takes you to them,' Barbary explained patiently. 'But you're his property now, you know. He's paying you good money.'

'I can see this isn't going to last for long,' Nell said ominously, glaring out at the innocent afternoon. 'At first, it seemed fun to have a holiday. But I'm *bored*!'

And despite the parties, the lovemaking, and the pleasure of Buckhurst's company, bored she remained. Some pleasure from her surroundings was possible, but she missed the theatre intolerably, longing for it from the moment she got up in the morning until the first people began to arrive in the evening. In the stimulating company of Buckhurst's friends she managed to forget the nagging sense of loss which haunted her and they thought her merry and witty, the prettiest little creature imaginable. Buckhurst, basking in the envy of his friends and the pleasure of Nell's company, thought himself a fortunate man.

This idyll, which he had thought would last all summer, came to an abrupt end after a mere three weeks.

'Why am I packing?' Nell flung at him when he came whistling into her bedchamber one warm morning at the end of June. 'Why? Because, Buck, I am bored and sick for London! I keep wondering who Hart has put into my parts, and whether the King is still in Town or whether the court has gone to Hampton or Windsor, and I roam the house reading old plays and practising old parts. I'm a London sparrow, and I cannot bear the thought of being away from my city one day longer.'

Buckhurst crossed the room and put his arms round her. 'My poor girl,' he said remorsefully. 'Is it I who bores you? Are you sick and tired of Sedley, and Barbary? If so, you've only to say and they shall move into the King's Head tomorrow.'

'It isn't them and it certainly isn't you,' Nell said, grinning at him. 'I've a lover more demanding than you could ever be; old London town herself. I cannot be happy away from her, and I simply must go back! But I'll never forget your kindness, Buck; I'll love you, a little, always.'

'Then I'll drive you back to town myself,' Buckhurst resolved. 'I had hoped my companionship might make up to you for the loss of the theatre, and the city. And if you truly loved me Nell, it would be so.'

'Perhaps,' Nell agreed with a sigh. 'But would you really *want* to be loved, Buck? If I loved you, I should want only you, and I should expect you to want only me. For ever and ever, you know. What do you think of that?'

'Oh!' Buckhurst said, digesting this. 'Well now, that sounds more like marriage than love, Nellie, and I have to admit that marriage is something I've spent most of my life avoiding. ... What are you laughing for, you impudent creature?'

'Never mind,' Nell said, her laughter gurgling into a hiccup. 'I love you in your way, easily enough, Buck. I love you for three whole weeks. Isn't that enough?'

'My love would have lasted the summer,' Buckhurst said with dignity, and then joined in her mirth. 'Never mind, love! We've enjoyed each other for three weeks, and we will remain friends all our lives. Is that a bargain?'

And there in the bedroom, with the half packed cases around them, they shook hands on their pact.

The first thing Nell did on arriving back in London, was to walk round to the theatre. They were rehearsing and Hart was on stage, tall and vigorous as ever, his curls standing on end in the heat, shouting, cajoling, and generally making his personality felt.

She sat quietly in the darkened auditorium and presently Meg Knepps noticed her and came running down the aisle between the benches, saying joyfully, 'Nellie, you're back! Is it for good, dear? No-one expected you so soon, so we've nothing but tragedies planned for weeks to come!'

'Quietly, Meg, I don't want Hart to notice me,' Nell warned her friend. 'Is he still furious with me?'

'Yes, he is,' Meg said. 'He still insists that when you return you shall be offered nothing.'

'Mr Killigrew won't let me want for a part,' Nell said, but her heart sank a little. 'Is he here, Meg?'

'Aye, in his room. You'd best go to him now, Nellie, whilst Hart is busy on stage. He's having a hard time with Stephania Uphill; she doesn't know the part of the Emperor's daughter, and he's lost his temper with her half-a-dozen times this afternoon already.'

But Nell had barely entered the manager's office, and greeted Mr Killigrew, when the door was flung open behind her. Nell, jumping, swung round to face Hart.

'So you've come back?' he said mockingly. 'Buckhurst got tired of you, no doubt. Well, why should *we* want his leavings? I told you, Tom, that I'd have none of her if she returned, and I meant it. Send her packing!'

'Nonsense, Charlie,' Killigrew said, scowling at his principal actor. 'You've taught her her trade too well for that! I want Nellie back and so do the audiences! Even in a few weeks we've lost the lead we had over the Duke's House, and that's because no-one can charm an audience like this little wench.'

'Then I shall go,' Hart muttered, without much conviction.

'I should be sad if you left me,' Killigrew said. 'But if you cannot work with Nell, then go you must.'

Hart scowled at Nell. 'Why did you come back?' He demanded. 'I suppose your keeper turned you off and you are short of money until you've found another? Why not try Madam Ross's, or buy yourself a basket and some oranges? You'd get a man that way without upsetting the company.'

'This sounds like personal animosity rather than the business reaction of an actor, Charlie,' Killigrew said. 'Suppose you and Nell settle your differences and then return to the work of running my theatre?'

'We'll settle them *here*,' Nell said firmly, reading the possibility of retribution in Hart's choleric glance. 'What do you want of me, Charlie? A signed promise to work at the King's for the next year? I'll give it, and gladly.'

'No need for that,' Hart growled. He smiled suddenly; not a pleasant smile, but a knowing, double-edged smirk. 'Tom, if she returns to work here, she takes the parts I lay down. Is that in order?'

'Well now, we've not got a comedy plan-ned for the next three weeks, they're all tragedies,' Killigrew said uneasily. 'Shall we change the programme, eh? Or we can ask Dryden to write her in a comedy part, or an epilogue to conclude the show with a good belly-laugh. How's that, eh?'

'No. If Nell is an actress, let her *be* an actress. I've been having the devil's own job with Stephania over this part. She's not the right age for it anyway, and she's having difficulty learning her lines. Peg Hughes was to do it, but she's gone off with her keeper, so I am doomed to Stephania, unless I can find a better.'

'What about Betty Ball?' Nell said. 'She's pleased you in the past.' He glanced at her sharply, but was at a loss to understand the cutting edge to her tone, since he had not the faintest idea that she had looked in on his amorous adventure with her friend.

'Bet is in the next play; quite a good part, and besides, she isn't a quick study,' Killigrew said, his expression amused. 'Come Nell, it's a fair enough offer. You *are* an actress, even though you hate tragedy; take the part like a man – or woman, rather – and do your best in it. At least you'll be paid, and I know you'll do better than most.'

'The audiences won't like it,' Nell said warningly. But even the thought of returning to the stage once more curled her lips into a smile. 'Oh well, if I must, I must. But you'll regret it, Charlie Hart!'

'Audiences are small at the moment in any case,' Hart said indifferently. 'The court is at Windsor and we're playing to wood half the time. You can get into practice for a long reign as Tragedy Queen, my dear!'

'Now, Meg, you must tell me all the news. I've not been absent a month, but I'm starved of gossip. Who is living with whom? Is the Duke still vacillating between Lady Denham and Arabella Churchill? What about La Belle Stewart?'

Meg chuckled. The two girls were sitting on one of the green lawns running down to the Thames, learning their lines whilst they enjoyed the sunshine. But now that the words had been committed to memory they continued to sit on the grass, content to gossip about small things and let their friendship renew itself.

'The Duke of York is *mad* for Arabella, and Lady Denham died, anyway,' Meg said. 'The King has taken her young brother, John Churchill, into his household to please Dismal Jimmy. As for the King himself, you know that La Belle Stewart married the Duke of Richmond for his money? The King's man, Chiffinch, is always procuring women for the King to sleep with. I was approached, but it was a strange business, and I said no.'

'Meg, how enchanting! You said no to the *King*?'

'Well, Buckingham approached me, and I was supposed to sleep with him first,' Meg admitted. 'I've got a lover of my own now, Nicholas Fakenham, so I don't want complications. Nicholas and I want to marry, one of these fine days.'

'I'm not going to start taking lovers again,' Nell said with finality. 'It only leads to trouble. Hart would see that I never got another comic part, and even Buck didn't much like being left, when it came to the point. He's put a story about that he grew tired of me! Did I tell you he is keeping my sister Rose? Strange, isn't it? He brought me back to London, almost weeping at the thought of leaving me, and whilst we were saying goodbye in my parlour, Rose breezes in. Hair all curled down to her knee, pretty riding habit, a saucy hat – I can tell you, she looked good enough to eat! She's three years older than I, so she's nearly nineteen, but she's a pretty creature. Well, he took one look at her and before I could introduce them, 'You've a look of Nell about you,' he says. And Rose, taking a quick glance out of the window at the coach and the match chestnuts, says "I hope that's a compliment, for you're handsome man yourself!" Next thing I know, they're walking out to the coach, his arm around her waist! And I never *did* find out why Rose came round to see me!'

'Any regrets, Nellie?'

'No, none. Rose is a fine girl, and has not had all the luck, despite being prettier than I. But I'll be a friend to Buckhurst to the day I die, for he was kind to me, in his way. It was kind to let me go without a fuss, when I found I wanted to return to London, and the stage.'

'And now that you're back? I know you didn't enjoy your last part – it was very tragic, was it not – but you'd not stop acting for all that, would you?'

Nell sat up, pushing back her heavy fall of auburn hair. 'Curse this sun, I shall freckle,' she said amiably. 'No, of course I won't stop acting! It's a pity I'm not a good tragedian but you know Meg, I'm too small, and happy looking. I've got a funny face, you might say. Every one should stick to their own trade, and mine's comedy, for better or worse.'

'Well, Hart can't insist on many more serious plays, that's one comfort. I bet you'll be acting in comedy again within the month!'

★ ★ ★

'A party? At Whitehall? Oh glory, how lucky you are,' Rose sighed, watching Nell bustling around the room, changing out of her costume. 'Buck has been very good to me, but he doesn't take me with him when he visits the King. Who else is going, Nell?'

'Several players from the Duke's including Moll Davies and Jenny Johnson, and most of the important players from the King's. It is to be a grand affair. The King is in disgrace with some of the nobles because of the peace with the Dutch. Imagine men being foolish enough to *want* war, but apparently they do! And Charles is depressed because he took the seals of office from Chancellor Hyde and would have impeached him, except he fled from England.'

'I thought Hyde did more than any other to get Charles his crown back,' Rose said, puzzled.

'So he did, of course. But he has grown more and more difficult and crotchety with the King, correcting him in public and treating him like a child. Poor Charles *had* to act firmly against him, but it went to his heart to do so.'

'I see,' Rose said. 'Is there any chance of including me in this party of yours, Nellie? I'd dearly love to see the King close to, and the little Queen, and Castlemaine and the rest.'

'Why not? You can pretend to be helping with the scenery and costumes,' Nell said.

So when the King's players entered the palace of Whitehall and lined up to meet the King, the sisters were together.

'There's Moll,' Nell whispered to Rose. 'Oh, look at her gown! It is cut so low I can almost see her belly-button! And so short it shows her ankles!'

Strolling over to Moll, Nell said affably, 'In costume already I see, Moll. Are you to dance a jig for the King, then? If you do, I'll warrant your breasts will fall out onto the floor.'

Moll eyed Nell with malice. 'At least the King doesn't treat me as a child,' she remarked in her pinched, careful voice. 'He knows a fine woman when he sees one.'

Nell nodded. 'Like Castlemaine, you mean? She might have been good once, but now she's getting to look kind of well-used, wouldn't you say?' And then, before Moll could answer, 'But I daresay the King likes his women a bit flabby. Makes him feel younger by comparison, perhaps. How old are you anyway, Mollie? You must be twenty – my, how old that seems to me, but then I'm only sixteen.' She turned back to Rose. 'You must let me introduce you to Mr Hart, sister.'

Rose, who had listened to the interchange with a smile, said approvingly, 'First blood to you, Nellie. *Didn't* she blush! And who is that man with the beautiful face, standing talking to the Duke of York? I've never seen anyone handsomer, upon my word.'

'That's the Earl of Rochester,' Nell said. 'He is beautiful, isn't he? And so innocent looking. But he is wilder and more of a libertine than Buckhurst, and that's saying something!'

'There aren't many innocents at court,' Rose said. 'But look, I think the men are getting ready to enact the play. What is your part?'

'We're doing a bit from *Twelfth Night*; I am Maria. After that, the Duke's players will do something by Beaumont and Fletcher. And then dear Mollie is to sing, and dance a bit.

And somewhere along the way we shall have supper.'

The evening went well, with the King watching all the performances keenly. He laughed louder than any, Nell thought, but he had a sad look in his eye. And as she strove to make him laugh during her piece, she thought she knew why women wanted to mother Charles Stuart.

Moll, with a soulful look in her eye and her heavy breasts hanging out of her gown, sang a sad little lament,

My lodging it is on the cold ground,
And very hard is my fare,
But that which troubles me most is
The unkindness of my dear.

And Nell, watching the King's face grow heavy with melancholy, thought he was remembering his fondness for Frances Stewart.

After a delightful supper, with the King cracking jokes, the players set about collecting their gear and preparing to take coach again for their respective lodgings.

'But Moll went with Chiffinch,' Rose said

gloomily, to Nell. 'Why didn't the King notice *me*, Nell? She isn't pretty, though she's got a fine singing voice. Why, her eyes pop!'

'He had ample opportunity to notice me,' Nell pointed out. 'But did he? Well, only in a fatherly sort of way! And I bet all he noticed about Moll were those great, pendulous breasts! But we've had supper with the King, and we've seen the inside of Whitehall, and that's a deal more than most people!'

They climbed into the coach, chattering and laughing, players who had had a successful evening doing what they most enjoyed. The coach driver knew where his clients lived, for his vehicle was often hired by Mr Killigrew to take the players about, and Rose had given him her address before climbing aboard, so every now and again the vehicle slowed to a halt, and someone got out.

As they neared Drury Lane, with only Hart, Lacy and Nell aboard, Hart turned to her, saying 'Will you leave the coach at your own lodgings, Mistress Gwyn? John and I are returning to the theatre to put the properties away. They went before us, in a separate coach.'

His tone was the cool, slightly patronising one which he had taken to using when addressing her now, and Nell replied, with equal formality, 'Very well, Mr Hart, the coachman knows my address.'

Lacy, who had been sitting quietly in one corner of the coach, suddenly bent forward with an exclamation, clasping his stomach. 'By God, but I've got a bellyache,' he said between gritted teeth. 'It was the oysters! I doubt I'll be much use to you, Hart.'

'Let us drop you off at your lodgings, John; we're just passing them,' Nell said, pressing her nose against the coach window. She pulled the cord and the vehicle lumbered to a halt. 'I'll continue on to the theatre and help Mr Hart with the props.'

'I can manage alone,' Hart said stiffly, but Nell, having accompanied Lacy to his lodging, climbed back into the coach and he did not remonstrate further.

Once back at the theatre they set about the task of unloading the coach of the few properties they had used at the palace. It was not hard work, but they carried in two thin wooden trees and a border of wooden marigolds, and then a basket of clothes. Working silently, the two of them stripped the coach and piled the stuff up in the green room, ready for real stowage in the morning.

'Are you walking in my direction?' Nell asked as they stepped out into the moonlight and shadows of Drury Lane once more. She knew that Hart could reach his lodgings by accompanying her, or by a different route.

'No.' Hart said curtly. He hesitated, but she turned from him with a quiet, 'Very well. Goodnight,' and set off towards her own home. She was not of a nervous disposition, but she knew that the area she would pass through was not a suitable place for a young woman at this time of night. A cat, crouching beside some stairs, miaowed and fled, bringing her heart into her mouth, and she remembered, uneasily, that she was wearing a light gown which shone milky pale in the moonlight so that she must be visible for the length of the street, and that she had a purse in her hand with the King's twenty gold guineas inside. But she stepped out briskly, trying not to think of the possibilities of rape and murder which lurked in every shadow.

Then she heard the footsteps behind her. Softly but steadily, someone was following her along the street. Once, she slowed and looked back, but could see no-one. She felt the skin on the back of her neck prickle, but told herself firmly that if it was a ghost, at least it would be interested neither in her purse of gold, nor her slightly tarnished virtue. And with such thoughts uppermost in her mind, she kept on walking steadily.

So did the unseen follower. But she kept on at the same pace until she saw her own front door, when she was unable to resist quickening her pace a little. She reached it, and fumbled for her key, unlocked the door, and slipped inside. Then she crouched behind the door, leaving it open the merest crack, and watched. Aha, it had *not* been imagination! He came soft-footed along the pavement until he was level with her door. He looked at it, then up towards her living room.

It was Charles Hart, and she knew the instant she saw his face in the moonlight that whatever he might have felt for her in the past, he had warmer feelings now. He was waiting for her light to go on so that he would know she was home safely!

With a little sob of relief she pushed open the door and ran into the road, clutching him so that he swayed and swore, not realising what had happened.

'What on earth...?' He said. 'Who...? What...?'

'Oh Charlie, Charlie, we've been such fools,' Nell said, putting her arms round his neck and standing on tiptoe to kiss his chin. 'Why didn't you *say* you liked me yourself? I've wanted you ever since I was a little girl of thirteen, selling oranges in the pit! And you've done nothing but treat me like a child, and teach me, and laugh at me. And when I proved myself a woman by going to live with Buckhurst you hated me, and scorned me. But all the time...'

Slowly, like a man in a dream, he put his arms round her. 'You wanted *me*?' he said in a wondering voice. 'Me? But I'm not a lord, nor a wit! I'm just a player. Far beneath *your* touch! You could have anyone, Nellie!'

She nodded, smiling mischievously up at him. 'Oh yes, far beneath,' she agreed. 'But

I love you, Charlie Hart! And you love me, I can see it in your face! Will you not come into my lodgings?'

He nodded, lifting her off her feet and striding into the house with her. 'Which way? Up or down?' He asked, nodding towards the stairs.

She laughed, nuzzling her lips into the side of his neck. 'We'll do both, in a minute,' she said. 'But my bedchamber is upstairs and there is a lovely soft bed there.'

He carried her up the stairs, and set her down just inside the bedroom. Whilst she drew the curtains and lit a branch of candles he watched her, his eyes tender. 'You're so small, Nellie,' he murmured as, her tasks finished, she allowed him to undress her. 'So small and white and tasty! It must be like making love to a child, or a fairy!'

She pulled him down onto the bed, smiling up into his eyes. 'I'm no child, Charlie,' she murmured. 'I may be small, but you'll find I'm a big girl now!'

# Seven

'Everything is going well,' Nell said, as she and Hart were waiting to be called on the first night of the new play, *The Mad Couple.*

Her affair with Hart was still on, but already it lacked the glow of rapture which had coloured the first weeks of their mutual passion, and she knew that Hart was eyeing other women and that she did not mind.

Our great love was the last tiny flicker of a childish crush, I suppose, she thought resignedly now. Then, cheering up slightly; but it was fun whilst it lasted!

She wondered vaguely if she would ever meet someone who meant everything to her, so that infidelity would be unthinkable on her part, and infinitely painful to her on his. She was beginning to doubt it. After all, she'd had two lovers now, and both had delighted her for a matter of weeks only.

133

Perhaps I'm shallow, she thought uneasily. Perhaps I can only enjoy brief unimportant relationships.

'If only the babies behave themselves,' Hart said uneasily now, referring to the children who were an essential part of the plot. He hated children or animals on stage with him, but had to admit that his own last scene, with the child in his arms, made good theatre.

'Oh, they will,' Nell comforted him. 'They've been so good! And think when the little boy pulled your nose at rehearsal yesterday. Even the cast laughed!'

'Yes, and if the baby pees all over me, the audience will howl with mirth,' Hart said resignedly. 'You've a way with babies, Nell, and I've none. But there, we'll see how it goes tonight.'

'If it goes well, and the King *really* laughs, perhaps he'll give me a great diamond ring like the one he's given to Moll Davies,' Nell said hopefully. '*And* a house in Suffolk Street! But I wouldn't retire from the stage if he gave me Whitehall! Moll Davies says she will, the indolent cat!'

'He didn't give her the diamond or the

house in Suffolk Street for making him laugh,' Hart said, adding, 'Or at least, it is not commonly believed.'

'Beginners, please,' shouted a voice, and the couple moved forward, Hart with all the excitement of a war horse scenting battle, Nell with a trace of the nerves which never quite left her.

'Ready, little one?' Hart said. 'We're going to make the King laugh until he cries. Remember?'

'Certainly I remember. And even Dismal Jimmy shall smile,' Nell said, referring to the Duke of York. She frowned at the stupid butterflies which seemed to be dancing up and down in her stomach. 'Let's hope that the children behave.'

And behave they did, for most of the play. Flushed with success and the laughter of the audience, Nell and Hart managed to control the children's high spirits, but they saw them off at the end of the last act with a certain feeling of relief. Now Nell and Hart had merely to sit on stage, whilst Hart recounted his doings, the baby in his arms. The baby, tired perhaps, or confused by the bright lights, began to whimper, then to wail, and finally, to roar. Hart stood up, trying to deliver his lines whilst frantically rocking the child and patting its back and Nell, unable to stop herself, burst into a peal of laughter – a peal which was echoed from the royal box where King Charles, the Queen, the Duke of York and sundry other important persons were holding their sides.

'Confound the brat,' Hart roared above the baby's cries. 'Can't *you* stop its mouth?'

'Oh, give him to me,' Nell said, whilst the child arched its back and fought, red-faced, against Hart's restraining arms. 'Bless me, I've never heard a child bawl like it!'

But before the exchange could take place, a termagent had swept up onto the stage, face red, eyes snapping. 'I'll thank you to leave orf ill-treatin' my little Thomas,' the child's mother screamed at Hart. 'What d'yer think you're a-doing of, hey? Come to Mam then, poor little lad, come to thy mother.'

'God, woman, you can't take it *yet*,' Hart said, exasperated. 'I have to walk off the stage and speak to it in a moment!'

'Oh do you, indeed? Well, 'e shan't be messed arahnd by the likes of you,' the woman said shrilly. 'You can manage wivout 'im! I needed money, so I said I'd lend 'im. But I dint mean for you to torment 'im like this!'

'Me torment *him*? I have done *nothing*,' Hart shouted, his face darkening. 'Your brat has tormented *me*! It slobbered all over my best shirt, it rubbed its snotty nose on my velvet sleeve...'

'And it did a pee down his best breeches,' supplied Nell, between gales of laughter. 'Let her take him, Charlie. Here, use this.' And she took a cushion from the couch and thrust it into his arms.

Fortunately, Hart had only a few more words to deliver before the curtain fell, but any amount of words, after such a scene, would have been wasted. The audience stood, cheering, called for the mother and her child to take a curtain call, shouted for Hart to display his pee-d upon breeches, yelled for Nell to 'laugh for us again', and generally showed their enjoyment of the entire incident.

When at last she was in her room removing her makeup and changing into a street dress, Nell was not surprised to find herself

137

the centre of attention. But what *did* surprise her was the hovering of a neat, middle-aged man with a deeply lined face, made remarkable by the shrewdness and humour of his bright little grey eyes.

He made no attempt to add his congratulations to the many being voiced, but remained in the background until most of her visitors had left. Then he made his way over to her. 'I am here on the King's behalf,' he said quietly. 'There is a supper party to be held at Whitehall. A small supper party. If you will agree to attend, a plain coach will be waiting outside in half an hour, pulled by grey horses.' He hesitated, eyeing her quizzically. 'It will be a *small* party,' he repeated meaningly.

Nell, who had recognised Mr Chiffinch from the moment she first set eyes on him, though she had never to her knowledge seen the King's personal secretary before, said apologetically, 'But I was to sup with members of the cast, Mr Chiffinch, and in particular, Mr Hart. I cannot just desert my friends.'

'Mr Hart is also invited,' Chiffinch said. 'He will accompany you in the coach. If, that is you will agree to come?'

'Oh, well, yes, I'd love to,' Nell said, aware that she was stammering but unable to collect her self-confidence.

As she pinned up her hair and quickly fastened her best necklace around her throat, Nell wondered why the rest of the cast had not been invited. How small, she wondered, was a 'small supper party'? At first she had feared it might be for two, and that she might find herself alone with the King. Not that I've any objection to that, she told herself as she wound her ringlets round her finger, it might be fun, and even if he wanted me to sleep with him, he is too much a gentleman to turn nasty if I found I had to refuse. She finished her preparations and pattered along the corridor to Hart's dressing room. Perhaps he might know more than she.

Hart, magnificently dressed in russet satin, greeted her with an exuberant hug. All his sulks over the misbehaviour of the baby had been cast aside long since. 'This is a great chance for you, Nellie,' he said, patting her cheek. 'To go from me to the King! I never thought I'd share my mistress with

Charles Stuart!'

'Share mistresses? Most likely he'll take me once, and never think about me again,' Nell protested. 'But I'm game, I suppose. Only think though, if I were to turn him down! *That* would be a thing, wouldn't it?'

'You mustn't even think it,' Hart said, his voice shocked. 'It would do us players no good. Why, he might even think I had had something to do with it!'

Nell laughed, but said frankly, 'You'd push me into bed with anyone for preferment, wouldn't you, Charlie?'

'Not anyone,' Hart protested. He held open the theatre door for her, gesturing to where the coach stood waiting. 'You don't want Chiffinch to hear you say things like that!'

He and Nell were quiet during the drive to Whitehall, Hart because he could not help wondering why he had been invited, if the King intended to seduce Nell, and Nell herself because, despite her brave words, she could not imagine what she would say to the King, if they were left alone.

But such fears were unfounded. The supper party was small, certainly, but the King and Lady Castlemaine were there, and Buckhurst, who smiled at her in a friendly fashion.

They sat down to supper almost immediately, at a round table. Nell found herself between Buckhurst and the King. Nell, watching from beneath her lashes as she began to eat, noticed that Barbara seemed very interested in Hart. As the warmth, the wine, and the excellent food began to banish her nervousness she saw that Barbara, also, seemed to grow bolder. She put her hand on Hart's knee to emphasise some point and did not remove it, and then Hart dexterously flipped the tablecloth over his leg, hiding the stroking movements of Barbara's still slender fingers. But Nell could not help smiling to herself at Charlie's expression of careful unconcern, hiding, she knew well, a very natural anxiety in case the King should take exception to his mistress's behaviour, and blame him.

'What are you smiling at, Mistress Gwyn?' The King said, and she turned to him, relieved to see that he was smiling too, plainly amused by the same incident. 'Why, I'm smiling to think of little Nellie Gwyn, of Coal Yard, supping with the King of England,' she answered. She looked up at the dark, lined face above her own, into the understanding eyes with their hint of perplexity, of sadness. 'I shall be seventeen years old in a few weeks. I've done a lot more than I ever thought I should!'

'Seventeen! I can remember, just about, what it felt like.' He gazed into space, his face sombre, then suddenly his expression lightened. 'Believe me, little Nellie Gwyn, it is better to be you at seventeen than it was to be Charles Stuart. But I think the meal is over for everyone now. Shall we rise?'

They left the table, Hart and Barbara still in animated, and somehow intimate, conversation, but the King did not move away from her as she half-expected, saying instead, 'Nellie – I may call you Nellie, may I not? – I've a fancy for a turn in the gardens before we settle down to chat. Will you accompany me? Buck shall fetch you a cloak.'

Buckhurst said smoothly, although he had not appeared to be listening, 'Certainly, Sir,' and left the room and Nell, glancing towards the small, golden silk couch where

Hart and Lady Castlemaine sat, said demurely, 'Of course I'll walk with you, sir. If your other guests have no objection, of course!'

'As you see, your fellow player is occupied,' the King said gravely. 'Barbara, poor dear, cannot but flirt with any good looking man. She's admired Hart on the stage for a while, and is doubtless delighted to find him as attractive close to.'

Buckhurst, returning with two cloaks over his arm, handed Nell one, saying, 'I will bid you goodnight now, Charles. And you too, Nellie, my dear. Be good!' And with that parting shot he left the room, laughing softly to himself.

Nell shook out the cloak but said, with dismay, 'This is not my cloak! I've one of my own, you know, which your servant took from me when we entered the palace. Hey, I've no mind to claim this, for mine is new, and costly!'

Charles said soothingly, 'It's quite all right, Nell, this is just a loan. It is soft and warm, and will protect you from the night air without any fear of your new cloak being soiled.'

Nell fastened it a shade reluctantly, noticing the perfume which rose from its dusky folds. 'I hope you don't expect me to roll on the ground in weather like this,' she said frankly, 'For I won't do it! Not for the King of Kings! It happens that I'm susceptible to head-colds and we're at the start of a successful run. I won't risk the play being ruined for the sake of a frolic in frosted grass!'

Charles, rather taken aback, said soothingly, 'Nothing of the sort. What tales you must have heard of me! And remember, I am no longer seventeen. I doubt I would survive making love in the open in mid-January. Seduction, at my age, needs to have all the trappings of civilisation, believe me!'

They were on the terrace now, and the King was gently closing the long glass doors through which they had come.

'Oh? Then you do intend to seduce me?'

The words brought him up short. The doors closed with a snap he had certainly not intended and he turned round, his mouth opening as though to refute the charge. Then he grinned at her, and put his arm round her waist. 'Buck was right. The merriest little lover, he called you! No, you delightful brat, I do not intend to seduce you! Or not the way you seem to mean. I merely thought I would get to know you better if we could talk in more ... intimate surroundings than those of the supper room. Does that explanation satisfy you?'

'I hope your intimate surroundings will include a fire,' Nell said, her teeth chattering as the icy wind whipped at her cloak. 'I would do almost anything to get warm, at this moment. God, what a cold night to go a-walking!'

'Well, it's only a short walk,' Charles said, leading her to a side door and holding it invitingly open. 'In we go. You'll be warm again in two minutes.'

He led her along a short corridor and into a small chamber where a fire blazed up brightly on the hearth and a branch of candles illumined the simple scene; the bed, with plain blue hangings, the round turkey carpet on the polished boards, the small, highly polished table with its barley sugar stick legs, with its burden of wine and glasses.

'This is never *your* bedchamber,' Nell said

disbelievingly, as he took her cloak and motioned her to sit on one of the velvet covered chairs, drawn up near the fire.

'Well, no. I've borrowed it from its true owner for an evening,' he said. Turning, he locked the door and crossed the room, throwing his cloak across the back of the other chair as he did so. 'The truth is, Nellie, that I've no desire to find Barbara suddenly knocking on the door and demanding entry, so I've fled my own chamber.'

'Would she do such a thing?' Nell asked. 'Surely not. It would be unforgivable.'

Charles shrugged, his eyes glinting in the candlelight. 'Barbara is a very unusual person,' he said dryly. 'Sometimes she does things merely to embarrass and annoy. She does not approve of actresses, you see.'

'But she approves of actors,' Nell rejoined, with a chuckle. Charles had flung himself down in the chair opposite hers, and now he held out his hands to her. Half shyly, half confidently, she moved across the carpet, and knelt by his side so that his arms went naturally around her shoulders.

'As you do yourself,' he reminded her. He

said, to the top of her head, for she was gazing into the flames, 'Charles Hart is your lover. Is he also the one you love?'

She moved round so that she could see his face, and he hers. 'No,' she said baldly. 'I thought he might be the right one for me, but ... no.'

He nodded, satisfied, and then stood up, helping her to her feet. Gently, experimentally almost, he pulled her into his arms and their lips met in a long kiss.

She pulled away first, saying breathlessly, 'How tall you are! I am on tiptoe, yet still I can scarcely get my arms around your neck. All those posters which were put up when I was first hatched were true, then! You really *are* a "black lad, all of two yards high".'

He chuckled. 'I'm blacker than you'd think,' he said. He tugged gently at the neck of her gown, like a child afraid to break a toy. 'How does this thing undo?'

'With all your experience in the undoing of females...' she began, then started to unfasten her bodice. 'But I suppose they undress themselves with the utmost eagerness, and you are not asked to unfasten so much as a piece of ribbon!'

He began to unbutton his own shirt. 'I don't know about that, Barbara has some funny ideas at times, I can tell you. But I find *actresses* are usually adept at dressing and undressing. Particularly undressing, now you mention it.'

Nell sniffed. 'Some actresses do little else, and would not have gained a place on the stage without a willingness to do so,' she said. 'But not me. I began too young, for I was only thirteen when I first took a part in Drury Lane, and by the time I began to interest men I'd already made a bit of a name for myself.'

'Aye. I took you for a child until recently. But something in your twinkling eyes made me wonder, and then Buckhurst said you were wasted on the stage, your performance in bed was so much finer. And I wondered, so I...'

Her chemise dropped to the floor and she smiled as he gasped, for the beauty of her body was something which she took entirely for granted, never dreaming that others were less perfect.

'What's the matter? You didn't think that because I play the lad on stage, I would have a body like one, did you? If so, no wonder you hesitated before inviting me to sup with you! And aren't you going to take your clothes off, too? A fine thing, that I must stand here naked, feeling ever so silly, whilst you are still in your breeches, with only two buttons of your shirt undone.'

He wrenched at his shirt and buttons popped, one of them hitting Nell's stomach as she stood there, tinted rose and gold in the firelight. 'Hey, your button hit me in my belly-button,' she protested. 'What a thing to do to me! I'd expected something *quite* different!'

'Oh, had you?' he said breathlessly. He stripped off his breeches and sat down in the chair to remove his silk stockings. 'And so you shall, my pretty!'

He stood up, as naked as she, and pulled her towards the bed. 'Come along, Nell, I must see if I can live up to your expectations.'

She climbed obediently into the bed, and lay smiling up at him, her dimples very much in evidence as she eyed his eagerness. 'You really *are* a long black boy, sure enough,' she said cheekily. 'I wonder how

Cromwell knew?'

He climbed in beside her and took her in his arms, giving a great sigh of pleasure as her warm body cuddled against him. 'Stories get around,' he murmured. 'By God, but you've beautiful breasts, girl, for all you're so small. We shall enjoy each other, I think.'

'All the best things come in small parcels,' Nell agreed. She moved against him, and feeling him stir, said, 'Or perhaps, not *all* the best things.' She watched his heavy lids droop over his eyes, and added thoughtfully. 'I've never been to bed with a king before. I wonder if it will be *very* different?'

'Stop talking, Nell, or you'll never find out,' he whispered huskily, and when she began to answer him back, stopped her mouth with his own.

When they were spent, and lay relaxed and dreamy, he asked, 'Was it different, Nellie?'

She considered him through slitted eyes, her mouth curving into its delightful smile. 'Different? The best I've ever known,' she said handsomely. 'Considering you're a king, you didn't do so bad.'

He laughed and cuffed her playfully, then

sat up and reached for the wine jug, which he had thoughtfully stood close to the bed. 'You'll find the second time is even better,' he promised. 'But that will have to be another day; our guests are waiting, perhaps even wondering why we are so long away. And besides, we don't want to return to find Barbara has eaten Charlie Hart alive! Do you want some wine before you get up?'

She shook her head, rolling out of bed at once and beginning to dress, without coquetry but with the grace and speed which she had learned in the theatre. 'I don't need wine to renew my energy,' she said as he filled his own glass. 'Overcome though I am at the honour done me, I've still got to get my beauty sleep. Rehearsals start early in the morning, you know. Or you should know, for though you may be my first King, I am most certainly not your first actress!'

'True,' he said, following her movements with his eyes. 'And I'm not your first Charles, either.' He chuckled. 'You could say that Charles the second is your Charles the second, Nellie!'

She shook her head, sitting in the chair

and pulling on her stockings. 'No, Charles the second is my Charles the third,' she corrected him. 'My Charles the first was Buck, and my Charles the second, Hart.' She glanced up at him, her eyes candid. 'Will you get dreadfully conceited if I tell you I wish you had been the first?'

He swung his legs out of bed and splashed wine onto the floor. 'No, I shall be in no danger of that,' he said. 'I wish it too, Nellie; but first or last, I enjoyed our time together.' He groaned. 'Oh God, my shirt's lost half its buttons, and there's nothing in here to fit me! But who's to notice a few buttons missing? Throw my coat over here, will you, lass?' 'Well? What happened?' Hart said eagerly, as they drove back to their lodgings.

Nell shrugged. 'What happened with you?' She countered. 'Did the lovely Barbara let you have your wicked way with her?'

Hart smiled reminiscently. 'What a woman!' He exclaimed. 'She had her way with me, if you want the truth. She's got a voracious appetite, I can tell you. I wouldn't want to satisfy *her* every night!'

'But did you? Satisfy her, I mean?'

He glanced at her, his expression suddenly

crafty. 'What if I did? You were off with the King somewhere. And not picking roses at this time of the year, either. I tell you Castlemaine's a fine woman, for all she's ten years older than you. A ripe armful. And the tricks she knows! I didn't know whether to envy the King or feel sorry for him!'

'Neither will make any difference,' Nell said. 'I like the King, Charlie. He's kind and full of nonsense, for all he can look so stern. I envy Castlemaine, not him.'

'Oh, I think the King is growing tired of Barbara and her greed and vanity,' Hart said. 'Yet he continues to support her and her children and pay her debts. She's had more than one lover apart from Charles, she told me so herself.' He glanced sideways at Nell, his eyes half apologetic, half pleased. 'She wants me to visit her again, in her own house.'

'That's good if you want it, Charlie, for you and I are finished, aren't we?' Nell said, a little ruefully. 'It was fun at first, but you're a man who likes variety, and I'm a woman who doesn't, that's the truth of it. I'd noticed your eyes – and your hands – wandering these past two or three weeks, so don't think

I've not! But it is natural enough, that you should enjoy one experience and then pass on to enjoy the next.'

'You're right, and I'm glad you're taking it so well,' Hart said eagerly. 'Youll not leave the stage because of it, though, will you?'

Nell threw back her head and laughed. 'Dear God, it is like asking me if I would stop breathing because someone had annoyed me!' She gasped at last. 'Charlie, Charlie, acting is my life! I would only stop acting for one reason, and that hasn't happened to me yet.'

'What is that?'

She leaned back in her seat, watching him in the dim light from the lantern outside the coach. 'I would stop acting for my true love,' she said seriously, and rather sweetly. 'But him I've yet to meet!'

The coach swayed round a corner and drew to a halt and Nell stood up. 'This will be my stop,' she said, opening the door and peering into the night. 'Yes, it is. Goodnight, Charlie. See you at rehearsal in the morning.'

'Goodnight, Nellie,' he said, half sadly. He watched her self-assured little figure walk swiftly into her house and shut the door, then told the coachman to drive on. It had been a pleasant interlude, he told himself, but already he was looking forward to what Castlemaine might bring. He chuckled as he thought of her strenuous and demanding lovemaking. A fine woman, and one who was rich enough for both of them. And if Nell had taken the King's fancy. He dismissed the thought. Sweet and comical though she was, was she of the stuff of which King's mistresses were made? She was neither greedy nor proud, and her attitude to lovemaking was one of laughter and tenderness rather than inventive lust. Charles might enjoy her once; twice, even, if she was lucky. But then he would go back to the well-born, self-seeking court beauties like Barbara. But she would be all right, would Nell.

'Nell, my pretty child, you continually amaze me! You are on the stage almost every day, rehearsing, going through your parts, learning the new play. You coach other players, you appear regularly at supper parties, you come quietly in and out of the palace, taking care of me and making me feel young and fascinating. And as if that is not enough, now I see that you've been secretly studying politics. It is all too much!'

Charles was sitting in his big leather armchair drawn up close to the fire in the small room he and Nell used sometimes when she visited Whitehall, with Nellie curled up contentedly on his lap. They had been discussing the possibility of an alliance with the French against the Dutch, or even with the Dutch against the French, and Charles had been considerably surprised at Nell's grasp of the subject.

'You are the one who works hard, not I,' Nell contradicted now, leaning her head gratefully against the King's shoulder. 'You play hard I know – riding, shooting, fishing, hunting, as well as tennis every morning before the rest of the court are even out of bed – but you work hard for England. You work for our good, you go short of money, and still you have to listen to their abuse, their intolerance, and their hatred. Yet you are always good-tempered, always kind. I never did worry my head over politics, or the affairs of the Dutch, or the possibility of a French alliance, until lately, but now that I *have* begun to look and listen, I'm horrified by what I see and hear.'

'The English are a proud and jealous people,' the King said sadly. 'They wanted a king, to be sure, but a puppet ruler; one whom the parliament could force to dance to their tune. But why their religious intolerance and bigotry should burn so fiercely...' he sighed, stroking the long auburn hair which Nell had loosed from its ribbon for greater comfort. 'Oh, I don't know.'

'Well, Catholics are bad,' Nell said, and chuckled when he cocked a quizzical eye at her. 'I'm sorry, but it is what we English have been taught to think!'

'And the Dutch, who are Protestant to a man?'

'Ah, we hate the Dutch because the Dutch are successful traders, and are therefore our rivals.'

'The French then, Nellie. What is wrong with the French?'

'They're Catholics. And Catholics are bad!' Nell said triumphantly. 'Everything comes back to money or religion, you see.'

'But English Catholics are *good*, my dear

little goose,' Charles said pensively. 'When I was hounded by Cromwell's men and it seemed that everyone's hand was against me, it was the Catholics who took me in, saved my life, succoured me, and in the end, helped me to escape. Not the righteous, prating Puritans nor even the English Protestants.'

'Well, I know that *now*,' Nell said comfortably. 'But I am *me*, and not the entire race of English. Your sister, the Duchess of Orleans, is a Catholic, which means you must find the French Catholics more to your taste than the Dutch. You love her very much, don't you? More, perhaps, than you love your women! But again you see, this is knowledge that I have, because I am lucky enough to be close to you. Ordinary people don't *understand*. And parliament just want to blame someone for everything that goes wrong, and...'

'Aye, you're right there. What they want is a scapegoat, not a ruler. But they've got me, for better or worse as it says in the marriage service, and they'll find it a lot more difficult to send me away than it was to bring me over. Here I am, and here I shall stay.' He brooded darkly for a moment, gazing into the leaping flames. 'Nellie, would you fear me, if I were to turn to you this moment and say, "Well, in point of fact, Nell, I'm a Catholic myself!"'

'No, but I'd fear *for* you,' Nell said frankly. 'The Duke of York has announced his conversion, and it hasn't made him either happier or more popular.'

'Very true. But you christened him Dismal Jimmy before he turned Catholic, and it's always been true of him,' Charles said. 'But why are we wasting time talking of religion, and parliament? What shall we do tonight? Apart from that!'

'There is a party at Killigrew's,' Nell suggested doubtfully. 'It will be in full swing now, but you will be welcome, as well you know. I believe Barbara will be there, though.'

'Oh, will she? Is she still sleeping with Hart? I don't see much of her, now.'

'So I believe. And what of La Belle Stewart, back in London and living at Richmond House? I thought she'd been forbidden the court.'

'So she has,' Charles said. 'I can have no

interest in Frances, now that she's a virtuous married lady, can I?'

'Of course not!' Nell said dryly. 'Meg Knepp was out late the other night, after a supper, and thought she saw you actually clambering over the garden wall of Richmond House! But you are so moral, sir, and so full of your own dignity, that no-one could believe such a tale!'

He coughed, patting her shoulder. 'Rumours, rumours,' he said uneasily. 'If you believed all the things they said of me, little one, there would be no room in your head to learn your parts!'

'Oh, I don't believe them *all*,' Nell assured him virtuously. 'Only those escapades which seem to be in character, such as this one!'

He laughed, capitulating. 'Oh well, I must admit I *did* visit the Duchess of Richmond. And it's a good thing I did, or I'd have spent the rest of my life believing I'd missed my one true desire. Now I know she's but a woman, a sweet, foolish woman, like the rest.'

Nell sighed, and cuddled closer to him. 'And what of loyalty, sir? Do you never think of that?'

'What, to a woman? Nell, I am loyal to *all* my loves. Is that not better than merely being loyal to one?'

'As long as you love us all, who am I to complain? I've a fine, funny part in the next play, sir, and when I'm playing it, I shall look up at you in your box, and know that your loyalty covers me and Moll Davies as well as La Belle Stewart and Castlemaine. And I shall pray that I may never treat you as Barbara has.'

'You are certainly not as greedy,' he said with a faint smile. 'You want so little, Nell! But it is a wonderful thing for me to know that you love me first and foremost for myself, and not for what I can give you.'

'It works both ways, sir! Not that there is much I can give you!'

'You give me yourself, which is the most valuable gift of all,' he said, kissing the tip of her nose. 'And I've decided I don't want to waste an evening at Killigrew's party when I could spend it with you. Let's go to bed!'

So they did.

# Eight

Old Mrs Gwyn trotted briskly along Lincoln's Inn Fields, looking up at the houses which lined the street. Fine houses, and in one of them her daughter had been installed by the King himself, or so Nell had implied. She searched the house-fronts, trying to guess which one harboured her daughter. Nell had said it was a pretty house, with blue painted shutters and hearts carved in the wood, and she had also said she would keep a look-out for her mother.

The road was tree lined and the wind, gusting as it moved the curly white clouds across the blue of the sky, was pulling the bright autumn leaves from the trees and whirling them along the gutter in a brilliant bonfire of colour. Somewhere, someone had a real bonfire too, and the faint thread of blue smoke, dispersed by the jovial wind, teased at the nostrils, reminding Mrs Gwyn that winter, and chestnuts roasting by the fire, and hot cakes for tea, were just around the corner.

But Mrs Gwyn, nothing if not practical, merely stepped over the leaves in the gutter and sniffed at the wood smoke and thought she would as like live here as anywhere. She rehearsed the speech she intended to make to Nell as she walked. Your sister Rose is wed to John Cassells, and she's expectations of a child at Christmas, and I've no wish to share a roof with a squalling brat, she would say. I'm past forty, she would say, and entitled to live with one of my children. You are doing so well for yourself, Nellie, and I wouldn't interfere with your life in any way. Only let me move into your spare room, and you'll not regret it. I can cook, and clean, and I'm handy with...'

'Hey, Ma!'

Her daughter's voice broke across her imaginings and she turned quickly, to find she had nearly walked past the very house she sought. Nell, looking pretty and capable in a blue woollen gown with cream lace at wrist and throat, was kneeling in the front garden, a trowel in one hand, a cluster of brown and shrivelled bulbs in the other.

'Come along in, Ma, but close the gate behind you. That dratted woman next door has a dog whose main aim in life is to kill my shrubs by peeing against them!' She pushed the bulbs into the crumbly dark earth and covered them over, patting them briskly, as though they themselves were small dogs. 'There! That was the last of my spring bulbs; we'll have a lovely display come March. Come indoors, Ma, and I'll show you the house.'

'Do you have to do the garden yourself?' Mrs Gwyn asked, following Nell over to the white painted front door. 'I should have thought the King might have got you a gardener whilst he was at it!'

'I don't have to garden, but I like it,' Nell said. She led the way briskly along a short passage, white painted to make it lighter, with a small oil painting of the King on one wall and herself on the other. 'And Ma, please don't go round saying "the King" in that way! I don't intend to make trouble for him by saying I'm his mistress – that Castlemaine suspects and gives me many a poisonous look – so I'd be obliged if you'd refer to him as Mr Charles, or as my keeper. Not that I'm fond of that expression, for it makes me sound like a dancing bear. But I prefer that even, to making trouble for him.'

'Well, as far as making trouble goes, I'm the last person to do that,' Mrs Gwyn said righteously. 'Though I'd not have thought it was making trouble to be acknowledged.' She glanced round at the doors leading off the passage. 'And this is a fine house, who-ever gave it to you.'

'You've not seen it yet; it is *beautiful*,' Nell said proudly. She opened the door before her and gestured to the room within. 'My kitchen. I just want to rinse my hands.'

A small, skinny girl, shaping cakes at the table, turned and stared, and Nell said, 'This is Lucy, Ma. She's a good cook for a littl'un. And she works hard to keep the house clean and tidy.'

'With no-one to help her? How can she keep the place as it should be kept?' Mrs Gwyn said, her voice rising. With desperate courage, she added, 'You need someone to help her, my girl! And here's me, with little enough to do in my own small place...'

The maidservant cut in. 'There's only the two of us, and Mistress Gwyn not 'ere 'alf the time,' she observed. 'I manages well enough, doesn't I, missus?'

'Indeed you do,' Nell assured her. She poured water from a tall jug into a round china basin and began to wash the earth off her hands. 'And how is Rose, Ma?'

'She's fit enough. Expectin' a brat come Christmas,' Mrs Gwyn said. 'And by that token, Nellie, I'd like to ask you...'

'Very well, Ma. In a moment. Lucy, would you bring coffee and some cakes into the parlour presently?'

Then the house had to be walked round, and admired, the stuff of the curtains felt and the price told and tutted over, the carpets examined and praised, the furniture exclaimed at, and by the time Mrs Gwyn was installed in the front parlour with a cup in her hand, she had almost forgotten her errand.

Almost, but not quite. She took a deep breath, smiled sweetly at her youngest child, and began upon her explanation. But no sooner had she given her ostensible reason for not wanting to live with Rose, than Nell said sweetly, 'What a pity you don't like babies, Ma, for I'm in the same condition! Yes, I'll be giving birth in late April or early May.'

With the wind taken completely out of her sails, Mrs Gwyn could only gape. Then Nell said, 'But I thought you might like to be with me, when the birth gets near. I shall have to leave the theatre, I suppose, when I'm too big, and it will seem strange and lonely, being here all day.'

'It isn't that I don't *like* brats,' Mrs Gwyn said hastily. 'Had two of me own, didn't I? But with Rose see, it would take up the spare room, her wanting a nurse and that, for the child.'

She did not feel it necessary to explain that Rose had also said some harsh things about the way her husband felt about having a drunken, loose-tongued old woman living in his house, but Nell, who had sustained a somewhat acrimonious visit from Rose already, appreciated the point.

'There is no man living here permanently,' she said now, to make it easier for her mother to accept the offer without losing face. 'So I shall have the child in with me, for a while at any rate.'

'And when you've a visitor, I'll keep well out of the way,' Mrs Gwyn said eagerly. 'Just you give me a room of me own, and tell me when to keep to it, and we'll get along fine.'

'You can have the small sittingroom at the back of the house,' Nell said. 'There's a bed in there, and Lucy will see you've everything you require. But Ma, I *mean* this. I won't have you embarrassing my friends with your remarks, when you've been drinking. Not any of 'em, whether they're from the theatre or the court. So when I've someone with me, you must keep to your own quarters. And if you come in drunk, or drink yourself silly when you're here, I'll lock you away, see? I won't have my house turned into a boozing parlour, for I know full well that's why you've been turned from your own lodging.' She took a deep breath and continued resolutely, 'And I'd best be plain, Ma, whilst I am about it. I won't have you bringing men in, nor trying to cajole young girls into letting you find men for them. I've heard from ... well, from other people, that you're not above that sort of thing, and I won't have it here. Is that clear?'

Mrs Gwyn also took a deep breath, to tell her daughter a home-truth or two, then exhaled without a word. Would it be worth it? It most certainly would not! Just for the sake of her pride she might lose a roof over her head.

'Yes, it's clear as anything, Nellie,' she said meekly. 'I'll move in in the morning.'

'You *are* pregnant, then?' Thomas Killigrew stared at Nell's waist, then smiled reluctantly at her. 'Where are you hiding it? I'd not have known, and it sometimes seems to me that actresses are pregnant more often than not. A mixed blessing, in fact! First, their love affairs keep them off the boards, and then their babies. I almost wish we were back in the days when Hart and Lacy simpered their way across the stage in roles such as yours.'

'And kept the King waiting whilst they shaved their beards?' Nell said mockingly. 'You can't mean it, Mr Killigrew! After all, a man playing Viola doesn't bring one extra member of the audience into the theatre, but my legs in hose bring scores!'

'Cheeky wench,' Killigrew grumbled.

'You're not very big, yet. When's it due? End of the summer?'

'No, in four weeks,' Nell said. 'If you could see me in hose, you would know. That was what decided me to tell you, and hand back my parts. Nothing looks worse than a pregnant young man!'

'Does the King know? You'll see that I'm sure he's the father, which is generous of me, for many of my actresses are hard put to it to name the begetters of their brats. But you are not one of them, Nell. You're a loyal little thing.'

'I'm not likely to seek other diversion whilst I have the King's affection,' Nell said simply. 'He's the only one for me, Mr Killigrew, even if I cannot be the only one for him.'

'You're an honest little soul, too,' Killigrew said. 'Now tell me, child, does Charles know?'

'Not yet. He's wrapped up in his sister's visit, and his plans for peace with France. And I don't want him to feel ... hampered, by me.'

'Why should he? His other mistresses have babies!'

Nell shrugged. 'Perhaps it is because I have always been independent. He's given me money, and presents, but I've always been able to keep myself on my earnings from the theatre. He knows, you see, that I love him because I want to and cannot help it, and not because I need his support. But I shall tell him this evening.'

He nodded, patting her shoulder. 'Good girl. It will give him pleasure, I'm sure. And though I shall have to change our programme, you shall still play the part when you are over the birth of the child. You will come back to us?'

'Of course! I shall need to be with the baby for a few weeks, but then I shall return to the theatre.'

She had planned to tell the King that evening since she expected him to call on her, but instead, Chiffinch's man arrived, to carry her to Chiffinch's house where a small, intimate supper party, such as the King loved to attend, was to be held.

But to her disappointment, the King was not present, though she had no doubt that he would send for her during the course of the evening. This thought sustained her until the last guests were calling for coats and hats, when a sour feeling of disappointment crept over her. But she shook the depression off and went to talk to her host.

'Where is the King?' She said quietly. 'Why has he not sent for me?'

Chiffinch shrugged, looking uneasy. 'He told me to invite you, and seemed certain that he would be present. But you'd best go quietly home, mistress. He must have business which he could not avoid.'

'Aye, business in skirts,' Nell muttered rebelliously. 'Confound it, and I particularly wanted to see him this evening!'

She was in her coach and about to tell Sears to move off when she heard the sound of feet thumping on the pavement, then the skid of gravel, and then a breathless hail. As her coachman called something incomprehensible, the door of the coach burst open and Charles II, King of England, stumbled across her feet and slumped into the seat beside her.

'Charles!' she exclaimed. 'What's the matter? Are you ill, or drunk? I've never seen you the worse for drink yet!'

'Certainly not drunk, but worn out with

172

running across from Whitehall to catch you up before you left,' he said. 'I was held up. To tell you the truth, it was Buckingham. He's getting difficult over this business with the French.'

'Buckingham? Your chief negotiator – if that's the right word!'

He chuckled. 'It is, but he isn't. Oh, I won't deny I've let him think he is the man of the moment regarding the possibility of peace with the French, but I am my own negotiator, Nellie! There is no money in the treasury and parliament is fickle as a woman, making a great deal of noise but unwilling to grant a single subsidy for the war they'd so dearly like to wage! No, we must have peace. France is powerful and we, at the moment, are not. And we must have peace with the Dutch too, for much the same reason. Our navy has been neglected, but theirs is strong. So peace it must be. And Buckingham is no diplomat, Nellie!'

The coach had covered the short journey to Nell's house whilst they talked, and now Joseph Sears shouted from the box, 'Are you gettin' out? I can't keep the 'osses standin' all night, you know!'

'Aye, we're getting out,' Charles said, grinning as he opened the door for Nell. 'A coach is no place for dalliance when you're my age!'

They entered the silent and darkened house together, but as soon as the door clicked open Lucy came running from the back of the building, to light candles and to conduct her mistress to her room. When she saw the King she stopped for a moment, round-eyed, and then silently handed Nell the branch of candles and the half-burnt taper and disappeared into her own quarters once more.

'We'll go straight to my bedchamber,' Nell said as soon as Lucy had shut the kitchen door behind her. 'The fire will be alight there, and the room comfortable.'

'And straight to bed,' Charles said, yawning hugely. 'I decided I was sick and tired of Whitehall and gentlemen of the bedchamber hovering. I shall stay with you until six o'clock in the morning, when I've a meeting for tennis, as usual.'

They undressed quickly and were soon snug in bed. Charles said sleepily, patting

Nell's rounded bottom, 'You're putting on a bit of weight at last, Nellie!'

'Yes, I am. But not there,' Nell said, glad of this opportunity to tell him her news. 'And the weight I am putting on will all be lost at once, if you understand me.'

'You're *pregnant*, Nellie!' He hugged her exuberantly, all of a sudden very wide awake. 'Dear God, I had begun to believe you were made of different stuff to my other mistresses, because you seemed impervious to my attempts. I'd begun to wonder if I'd lost the knack of fathering brats. When is it due?'

'In about four weeks.'

He whistled softly in the darkness. 'And my sister arrives in England about then. You'll not be able to see her. A pity, you would have loved Minette and she you.'

'I may give birth early,' Nell said hopefully. 'Could you not bring her to see me, if I am still abed?'

'She isn't coming to London. Her detestable little pervert of a husband has seen to that. He didn't want her to come at all, but has allowed her just one week. We shall meet at Dover, and shan't waste time travelling all the way to Whitehall.'

'Then I shall see her on her next visit,' Nell said determinedly. 'And now, sir, let us either go to sleep, or...'

He put his arms round her and chuckled at the swell of her stomach against him. 'Practical, sensible little Nellie!'

'Isn't he beautiful, Charles?'

The King stooped and looked into the dark, self-absorbed little face of his latest son, and said, 'Very beautiful,' absently. He held out a finger and the child's tiny fist bumped into it and clutched. The absent-minded look left Charles's face and real affection took its place. He lifted the baby gently from the cradle, humming a snatch of some song popular at court, and began to walk up and down, smiling at the child. Nell, watching from the bed, said softly, 'You are more used to babies than I! And how did your sister's visit go?'

His face lit up, as it always did when Minette was mentioned. 'It was marvellous to see her again, Nellie! She is the prettiest, sweetest creature. She is devout, and clever, and she has the kindest heart. But the time soon sped by, and she is back in France, now.' He sighed, half-comically. 'And she had the prettiest maid of honour! Louise Queroalle. A child of nineteen, with soft, pouting little lips and great, gentle eyes. A dove of a girl. I suggested Minette might leave her as maid of honour for the Queen, but she wouldn't. Said she had responsibilities, and was *in loco parentis* to the maid.' He sighed again. 'So I accompanied my dear little sister halfway across the channel, and miss her deeply. I pray God her next visit may be soon.'

'Whose visit? Minette's or Louise's?'

He laughed, and held his dark face against the baby's for a moment. 'Minette, of course. I don't deny Louise caught my fancy, but there are plenty of pretty women about, God knows. There is only one Minette.' He glanced into the child's crumpled face. 'He's sleeping, Nell. Shall I put him back in his cradle?'

'Yes, please. I shall be up and about soon, and able to entertain you once more in quite my old way.' She cocked a meaning eyebrow at him. 'That will be more satisfactory than these fatherly visits, won't it?'

'Of course,' he said, but when he had gone she remembered, with an ache in her heart, the 'plenty of pretty women' he had mentioned. But her downheartedness didn't last long. She smiled to herself, vowing that as soon as her lying-in time was over, she would show him what he had been missing. And that would make him forget other pretty women, no matter how they might throng about him in her absence!

Chiffinch let her in. It was late, and she saw with concern that his face was grey with fatigue. 'He's not sent for you,' he admitted as soon as she was safely in his small sitting room. 'But I had to do something, Mistress Nell! Ever since the news of his sister's death he's scarcely eaten, scarcely spoken. He says he must forget, but I don't think he's capable of forgetting just because he *wants* to. Confound it, Mistress, I don't think he does want to forget. He is crushed and bewildered by his loss.'

'Then how am I to go to him?' Nell asked uneasily. 'I cannot go to his chamber un-invited, the Queen might be with him, or ... or anyone.'

'I thought I would tell him a woman awaited him in my room. You know, the room where you and the King first lay together. I sometimes bring women for him there. And the strange thing is, I think he would go to meet a stranger, though he will not see his friends. Will you agree?'

Swallowing the pain and humiliation that must come when she thought of him with other women, Nell said, 'Very well. But if he refuses to see me, will you give me warning so I may go home again? My child is with the nurse, but I don't like leaving him for too long.'

He nodded, impatient now that his goal seemed in sight. Together they went to the room and he left her in remembered candle-light whilst he went to talk to the King. Nell, sitting in the chair by the fire, thought of Minette's death, which had come so un-expectedly that cries of poison had been hastily suppressed. They had accused the Duke of Orleans' latest favourite, but no-one in England believed it. They said that Minette had been delicate from a child, and that she had seemed pale and far from well during her time in England.

And now? She had come at Chiffinch's request because she longed to see Charles so fervently, and because she believed that he had called for her. His son, it seemed, meant nothing beside his grief, for he had not visited her since he heard the news.

Sitting quietly before the fire, she planned a witty speech to make him laugh, a wild gaiety which would take the sadness from his eyes for a moment. Anything but tears and reproaches, for he must have had his fill of them.

And then the door opened and he stood there, his eyes only taking in that she was there, neither welcoming nor repelling.

She flew into his arms, tears running down her cheeks, and he held her tightly, not speaking, just patting her back as her sobs subsided.

'I've been so *lonely*,' she muttered at last. 'I've wanted to see you, to talk about our son, but I've not dared to come to you whilst you have endured such pain and grief. I know you didn't send for me, but I felt I would stoop to *any* trick, just to see you for a moment. Oh Charles, forgive me!'

He held her lightly, rocking her in the cradle of his arms. 'Forgive you? It is I who need forgiving,' he said wryly. 'Forgetting the mother of my son, leaving you both without my support whilst I struggled with an emotion as useless as regret. But that is past, Nellie. It must be past, or I shall never find the strength to carry on.' He smoothed her hair gently, then turned her face up towards him. 'What, still weeping, Nellie? My sunshine girl, who never cries? Come, let me see you smile!'

She smiled shakily, her eyes still large with tears. He looked down at her, his expression arrested. 'God, you're beautiful,' he said. 'And I've no portrait of you. I'll send Lely to your house and he shall paint me the most beautiful picture of you, so that even when we can't be together, I shall still be able to see you.'

'How will he paint me? With my stage paint on? In costume?' Nell asked, her face brightening. She sniffed and wiped the last of the tears away unselfconsciously with her cuff.

He began deftly unfastening her bodice, smiling at her as he did so. 'He will paint you as I like to see you best,' he said, and the old, wicked smile lit his dark face. 'And presently you shall tell me about our lad, but now...'

# Nine

'You were so *funny*, Nell! We laughed until the tears ran down our cheeks. But I'm afraid Louise didn't join in our amusement. She was offended, I fear.'

'Good!' Nell said heartily. 'I don't act to make *her* laugh, Charles! Why should I? Louise de Queroalle is a damned, simpering Frenchwoman and even if *you* won't acknowledge why the French King sent her over to your court, the rest of England does! A French whore this time, to seduce him to the Catholic church first and then to the French alliance, they're saying in the streets.' She snorted. 'And it's my belief that it's the truth. A woman of good breeding she calls herself, yet she sits next to you in her box with her tits hanging out of her dress, looking as though butter wouldn't melt in her mouth.'

'You're jealous,' Charles said with un-ruffled cheerfulness. 'And you may think her shameless, but she won't yield her virginity to me, at any rate! And you must not tease her! It was bad enough when you parodied poor Moll Davies's lovely song, but I won't have Louise offended. If you continue to make fun of her, I shall be annoyed!'

'Oh, and you must not be annoyed! Look what happened to that priggish Coventry when he had the affrontery to tell parliament that you were not so much a patron of the theatre, as of actresses! Someone slit his throat one dark night when he was walking home down Suffolk Street. And you visit there, sir, when you're bored.'

'I don't only visit Moll when I'm bored,' Charles said coolly. 'And anyway, why should I not visit her? Not that I do. I'm too occupied trying to keep the peace between you and Louise. Nellie, you naughty child, why can you not regard my fair French dove with complacence? I should love you the more for it.'

'Well, it's partly because she's so *stupid*,' Nell said. 'If she had not worn a ridiculous hat at court, then I would not have worn an even more ridiculous one when I recited the epilogue, and then no-one's feelings would have been hurt. Oh, I know she says I am making fun of the French ambassador, and thus of her. And another thing is her giving herself airs. I cannot *abide* such behaviour. Always talking about my uncle the duke and my cousin the prince, yet if all this were true, why should she come to this court and lie on her back for *you*? She might legally marry a great French nobleman, or something. And then she's got no conversation. When I'm at Whitehall I find more pleasure in chatting to the *Queen* than I do...' She stopped, her eyes rounding. 'Now that *was* rude,' she admitted, stricken at how far her tongue had carried her into indiscretion. 'And I'm sorry for it, Charles, because the Queen is always kind and polite to me. But her English is still foreign sounding, like Louise's, I suppose, which must have made me say it. Charles, I didn't mean to be rude to the Queen!'

'No, perhaps not,' Charles said sternly, but with twitching lip. 'But you see where your cheekiness can lead you, Nellie! And I'm warning you, once and for all, that I won't have Louise upset. Do you understand?' She was silent, and he crossed the room and took her chin in his hand, tilting her head so that she was forced to meet his eyes. 'If you continue, I shall not visit you,' he threatened softly. 'And *that* would mean we should both suffer.'

Her lips trembled, but a smile broke through. 'Pooh to that,' she said scornfully. 'If you stop visiting me then I shall let Louise have it with everything I've got. If you think I've been unkind to her already, you just don't know how dreadful I could be. Besides, you could not be so cruel as to punish my Darkie-baby who has done you no harm, and who loves your visits so?'

He smiled tauntingly, still holding her captive. 'There is visiting and visiting,' he reminded her. 'I should still visit Darkie, of course, but I cannot share my bed with a woman who deliberately upsets Louise. Especially before I've made her mine,' he added ingenuously.

'Oh, I'll be as nice as I can, then,' Nell said, capitulating abruptly. 'But it seems to me that all the niceness is on one side!

Barbara was *hateful* to me, Charles, and well you know it, but you still urged kindness upon me. And now this one holds up her nose so disdainfully, and makes the most spiteful remarks in her tight little voice, and you tell me that I must be kind. I'll bet you've not given her similar instructions.'

He was remorseful, especially when a tear slid down her cheek. 'Poor little one,' he said, holding her tenderly. 'It is quite true that I've not told Louise to be nice to you. But she's not got your generosity, nor your quick wits, and she isn't very popular with the people, either. Here, I've been meaning to tell you, I've got you a house! A whole big house of your own, not part of one, like this. Will that be a sufficient reward for being nice to Louise?'

'A house!' Nell clapped her hands, her eyes slitting with pleasure. 'Where is it, Charles? Is it a big house? A handsome one? Oh, and is it near Whitehall? Don't say you are going to depress my pretensions by giving me a cottage in the country some-where, where you need hardly ever see me?'

He laughed, and pinched her chin. 'Scarcely, for that would not be in my own interests. No, it's a neat little house in Pall Mall, very close to the palace. I shall be able to send for you, knowing you'll be with me in no time.'

'That sounds more like it,' Nell said. She gave a little jump. 'A house of my own! I shall move in as soon as I have the keys and the freehold.'

Charles said a little uneasily, 'Well, as to that, I don't think it is freehold; none of the houses along there are, you know. But it's a fine house, and the leasehold...'

'But you said when you found me a house, it should be mine, and Darkie's after me,' Nell objected. 'You made a joke about it, you know you did! You said you'd held the freehold on my...'

'Yes, you're right, I remember now,' Charles interrupted hastily. 'Very well, little one, a bargain's a bargain, and you shall have your freehold. But remember, be nice to Louise!'

At the new house in Pall Mall, a party was in full swing. Candles shone, women talked and laughed and pulled pretty faces, men told stories, roared with mirth, and drank deep. Nell, standing watching for a moment, congratulated herself upon her evening.

It had begun well, with a trip to a see a new comedy at the King's House, newly built after it had been destroyed by fire some months earlier. She had not acted since moving into the new house, and wondered whether she would do so again, for the King became restive whenever she mentioned reading a new part. Charles was here and annoyed, for once, with Louise, who had objected to being invited to a party given by 'that common little strumpet'. 'She looks as fine as any lady,' Charles had objected, and 'Yes, but she swears like an orange girl,' Louise had replied, making Charles slap his leg and laugh saying that Nell couldn't deny that, damned if she could.

And despite the fact that she was heavily pregnant, Nell knew she looked good. Her hair shone with health and had been prettily curled instead of falling loosely to her waist. It suited her, and through her ringlets was threaded a gold coloured satin ribbon which matched the gown she wore. Sitting in the box at the theatre, laughing helplessly as the mad, delightful plot unfolded on the stage, she had noticed how Charles looked at her, and was glad.

And not only the King was admiring, this evening. His eldest bastard son, James, Duke of Monmouth, had been unable to take his eyes off her. She was not overly keen on the young man, only a year her senior, who snubbed her sometimes in a drawling, superior voice which irritated her, but she knew that if *he* admired her, she must be looking her best. The gown was tactfully cut, falling straight from the proud curve of her breasts to her toes, and hiding the swell of her laden stomach.

After the theatre, they had returned to her house for cards, supper and gossip. The Duke of York, his heavy, self-righteous face flushed with drink and the warmth of the room, was leaning over Arabella Churchill, advising her how to play her cards. One hand pointed to the table, the other fumbled with Arabella's beautiful, firm breasts, until Nell could have laughed aloud at the other girl's obvious embarrassment. Dismal Jimmy must think we are all as drunk as him, and cannot follow his movements she thought, and caught Charles's eye. He came over to her side, too polite to break up her party but obviously eager, now to see the end of it.

'How soon shall we be rid of 'em?'

She shrugged. 'What, Charles? Do you intend to stay with me, when I'm so fat and hideous, and Louise so slender and willing? I know she's pregnant too, but it scarcely shows yet. You'd best not disappoint her tonight!'

'Disappoint her? She'll be delighted to be spared the whole crude business of satisfying me,' he said lightly. 'And besides, her "condition" is all she will talk about. Here I am, straining every nerve to get into her, and when I do, what happens? She conceives, and thinks she mustn't be touched by a man until after the birth.' He snorted. 'But I've had that slut Barbara speak to her, so perhaps she'll change her mind soon.'

'Well, I'd tell her, except of course that she'll say it's one thing for an orange girl, and quite another for a member of the aristocracy.'

'Would you try?' Charles said, not un-hopefully. 'You've been good with Louise lately. She has been very difficult, but you've not been rude to her for a month.'

'It must be my condition,' Nell said. 'Drat, I hope I'm not going soft in the head as well as hard in the belly! But the answer, of course, is that I'm only rude to Louise when she is rude to me, and she's polite, now she's with child. Do you know why?'

'No. Why?'

'Because she thinks it will be the death of her, and she doesn't want to go to heaven with mortal sins fighting for her soul.'

'Really?' Charles said, much struck. 'Poor Louise, perhaps I had better stay with her tonight. After all, it will mortify her dread-fully if she realises I am not leaving to return to Whitehall with her.'

'On the other hand, if I slip out to my coach and drive round to the side entrance of the palace after I've given my girl a hand to clear up here, I could be with you in, say, an hour,' Nell suggested.

And in the end, that was what she did. The party gradually broke up, Louise with a formal smile on her baby face, thanked Nell and left, hanging triumphantly on to Charles's arm, and Nell began to clear the room with Lucy's help, thinking that if Louise could know her plans for the next hour, it would have wiped the smug look off her face quicker than the most carefully planned insult.

Mrs Gwyn did not come through to clear away the remnants of the supper and so Nell took a hot drink through to her room, but her mother was curled up beneath her blankets, snoring stentoriously. She stood for a moment, listening to make sure that her mother's sleep was genuine, for she would have hesitated to leave the house for a few hours with the servants dead tired and her mother searching for drink. But the sleep was genuine; Mrs Gwyn had probably managed to get at the brandy and would disturb no-one until morning and Mrs Biddenden, Charles's nurse, would see that no harm came to Darkie, as she and the King invariably called their son.

When the rooms were straight and she herself ready to leave, she hesitated over calling her coachman. It seemed ridiculous, with the palace so close, and in any case,

Sears would have gone to bed by now, sure that he would not be needed. But there was Sally, the kitchenmaid, or Lucy, who had risen to a higher position in Pall Mall because she had been with Nell so long. Here, she was a personal servant, helping Nell with her clothes, making and mending, and leaving the more menial tasks to the cooks, the butler, and the other servants.

Making up her mind, she went through to her bedchamber, calling 'Lucy!' The girl came out, obviously expecting to help put her mistress to bed, but Nell said, 'I am going over to the palace for an hour or so. I shall want you to accompany me, and wait until I return. You can nod off to sleep in one of the withdrawing rooms, and then I shall have someone to walk home with.'

Lucy made no demur, merely fetching thick cloaks, but Nell thought they were both half asleep as they let themselves out of the front door. But the cold winter air woke them up and they stepped out briskly, glad of the faint starlight which illumined their way.

'When we get to the palace, I'll show you where to wait. Don't talk to anyone, for though it sounds strange, there are some odd people at Whitehall, even in the middle of the night. I'll return for you as soon as I can.'

As they began to cross the gardens she asked herself, for the first time, what sort of a court it was when she, a whore from the backstreets of Drury Lane, was afraid of the type of man her little maidservant might meet there. It is not the King's fault she thought, immediately loyal to her lover, for he would not hurt anyone, would never so much as take a slut off the streets against her will. It is the others, who behave so badly, and he does nothing to punish them for their behaviour. She thought about Captain Blood, who had very nearly succeeded in stealing the crown jewels. The King had interrogated him personally and must have realised what a rogue the man was. He had held him imprisoned for ten weeks and had then released him. To work as a government spy, Charles said, yet the man was forever to be seen around Whitehall, or any other place where the King, and important persons, might be found. And he was not the only one. Men from whom she felt safe enough herself, with her experience and her quickness of perception, but whom she knew she would not like poor Lucy to be faced with.

'I shall leave you with Mr Chiffinch,' she said to Lucy, coming to a sudden decision. 'He won't be abed yet for the King will have told him to stay up to let me in. You will be safe enough with him.'

'Very well,' the girl said. She yawned. 'I hope Mr Chiffinch won't take it amiss if I fall asleep, for I'm mortal tired!'

'I am hoping the same of the King,' Nell said, with a chuckle. 'Imagine my shame and his disappointment if I fall asleep the moment my head touches the pillow!'

Laughing together, the two women tapped on the side door and were let into the palace by the discreet Chiffinch.

'It is late to come a-visiting Mistress,' Chiffinch said, looking at her pale face with some concern. 'You must lie in tomorrow morning.'

She smiled at him, grateful for his concern. 'May I leave my woman with you, Chiffinch? I don't suppose the King will keep me long, tonight.'

But the dawn was lightening the sky

before she and Lucy made their way back to the house in Pall Mall.

Nell's second son, christened James, after the Duke of York, was born on Christmas Day.

'What a way to celebrate Christmas,' his mother said when, damp and exhausted after a short but painful labour, she lay in bed with her new son in the curve of her arm.

Charles, who had come to her as soon as a servant told him of the birth, leaned over and kissed her, taking the child from her and saying, 'There is a precedent, little one! Not that I claim any of the Virgin's qualities for you, for I'll warrant you swore your way through your ordeal, as I've heard you swear your way through so many.'

She smiled wearily at him, pushing back the damp, reddish hair from her brow. 'Poor Charles! Your women spend half their time pregnant and the other half recovering from the birth. And what are you supposed to do then?'

'There is always the Queen, of course,' he said. 'She does nothing so disrespectful. She is always mine to command.'

There was a short silence. Then Nell said softly, 'Oh, my dear! You would love the Queen to bear children as much as she would, and all your sons, fine, dark Stuart sons, can mean nothing to you because they will never bear the burden and the pride of the crown.'

'And a good thing too,' he said sharply. 'God knows, Monmouth is eager enough to feel the weight of it. And he'd make a much better king than dismal Jimmy, but it would never do. I cannot perjure myself and swear I married Lucy Walter when I did no such thing. And sometimes, I think there is enough of her in him to make him – unsuitable – as a ruler.'

'What was she like?' Nell asked. Charles sat himself down on the counterpane and passed the child to her again.

'Well, she was pretty; very pretty. A little round, naughty face, heavy lids over dark eyes, bee stung lips. Have you not seen portraits?'

Nell shook her head.

'Well, she was pretty. But determined, too. She was sweet and pliable when we first met, and when the child was young. But later, as she grew older...' He shrugged. 'Women change, and she wanted more than I could offer her. Did I take a young, beautiful girl and change her into a greedy, selfish woman? I don't know. Perhaps.' He stood up sharply, stretching and yawning. 'I'm not much of a man, Nellie, but I'm loyal to my friends. Don't let anyone tell you differently.'

'What do you mean?' Nell asked. 'No-one could convince me you are anything but good.'

'What about Monmouth? Has he never tried to persuade you to tell him how I am going to act? Is that not implying that I might act in a way which might discredit my country in some way?'

She flushed, remembering Monmouth's attempt, only a few days previously, to persuade her to spy on Charles for him, and to pass on any chance remarks on his foreign policy which the King might make when in her company.

'Your favourite son, sir, is a self-opinionated pup, but he can be very unpleasant indeed if flatly sent about his business. He is happy enough to call me whore behind my back when I'm civil to him, and to my face when I'm not! What do you advise me to do, then? Tell him I'll not help him, and have his enmity? You are always careful to keep your friends, so why should not I? I would tell him nothing even if I could, and you know very well that you're close as an oyster with everyone. Not just with me and Louise and Barbara, Charles, but with *everyone*! Buckingham thinks himself hand in glove with you, so does Clifford and a dozen others. The truth is you're hand in glove only with yourself. But to tell that to Monmouth would merely earn me sneers and hatred, for he'd not believe me. Come, tell me, what would *you* do?'

He smiled, his dark eyes glinting at her. 'You're sharp as a needle, Nell, whatever Louise may think! They won't understand, these women, that I want them for their charms in bed, and not for their brains! Well, to be frank, Barbara has no brains and Louise precious few. But even if they were as brilliant as ... as...'

'As yourself?'

He flung up a hand, acknowledging the

hit. 'Aye, as myself. *And* as modest! Even if they had the minds of ministers of state, I'd not want their advice or their warnings. I must go my own way as far as in me lies.' He glanced down at his boots, flicking his gloves against his hands. 'God knows, with parliament pushing when I cry pull and pulling when I beg them to push, it is little enough of my own way I have, without lies and deceit.'

'Not that you've the slightest objection to using both,' Nell said provocatively.

'Not the least in the world. And by the way, young woman, just precisely what did you say to Louise on the subject of sex after conception? Even the mention of me joining her in bed sends her into strong hysterics. I thought you would help me, you vixen.'

Nell, who had retired precipitately beneath the blankets at the first mention of her talk with Louise, replied in muffled tones, 'I told her I'd heard of a girl who let her man bed her after conception, and she conceived again and again, and gave birth to a *litter*. I thought it might make the bitch think twice about letting you.'

Charles threw back his head and laughed,

bringing an appreciative titter from beneath the blankets. 'Vixen!' he gasped out at last. 'What hell my life has been made because of that foolish tale! Come out from under there and tell me what I should say to Louise to banish such ridiculous fears?'

'You might try telling her that Nell had only one baby, despite repeated ... applications,' Nell said, still keeping beneath the blankets for safety's sake. 'But she'd probably say it was different for a common woman.'

'I'll tell you what she says tomorrow,' Charles said, mopping his eyes. 'Well, at least you've made me laugh, Nellie, and I didn't feel much like laughing when I arrived.'

'Isn't that what I'm for?' Nell said, sitting up in bed, her cheeks pink from the heat beneath the blankets. 'And by the same token, I take it I may retain Monmouth's friendship by telling him I'll help him, and then not doing so?'

He smiled at her with real affection, standing by the door now, pulling on his gloves. 'Of course you may,' he said gently. 'There is no-one to whom I would rather trust state secrets than yourself, if I had to trust them to anyone, little Nellie. Take care of yourself. And of my sons.'

And he was gone, whistling down the stairs and back to the palace, leaving Nell alone with her boys.

# Ten

Nell's life at court had been considerably brightened of late by the arrival of an old friend. Peg Hughes, who had first taught Nell to read and whose acting had so charmed her, had been mistress to Prince Rupert of the Rhine for some while and had borne him a daughter, but she had recently been much at Whitehall with her lover and she and Nell had been able to renew their old friendship.

And now the two friends sat in the privy chamber at Whitehall, doing their embroidery and discussing Louise.

'The King has made her Duchess of Portsmouth, yet he still seeks my bed. She has "headaches", and she is "unwell"; she feels sure he won't insist on forcing his presence upon her ... any excuse. But I don't mind, for it sends Charles to *my* bed and whatever my faults may be, few can be found with my performance *there*.' She chuckled. 'Yet Charles just says he understands his sweetheart's holding back, and that her surrender, when it comes, is all the sweeter. She's terrified of having another child, of course. Said the first birth, for one of her delicacy and breeding, was a horrific experience, and one she has no desire to repeat. I actually told her, much though it went against the grain, that a second birth is generally held to be much easier than the first but it made no difference. So I satisfy Charles whenever he wants me, because I love him and want to please him. And am called a whore by his son. And Louise, who only satisfies him when her own lust becomes unbearable, is thought fine, and sensitive. No justice, is there?'

'Not much. How will Louise feel when this uneasy alliance with France breaks up? It cannot go on much longer you know, the pretence that we are allies. My poor Rupert fought alone during the sea-battle off Texel because the French refused to come up and support him.'

'I heard, Peg. What will it mean, do you

suppose? Will the war against the Dutch end, or will we fight them more furiously still to prove that we don't need the French?'

'Rupert thinks the war will end,' Peg said. 'And with James marrying Mary of Modena in the autumn, perhaps there will be less talk of war and more of peace.'

'I don't see why,' objected Nell. 'He was bound to marry someone and Mary is an Italian, so it should make ... oh look out, Louise is coming over.'

Louise came regally towards them. Her beauty was enhanced, if anything, by the weight she had gained so that her breasts were plumper than ever, her movements slower and more graceful. She smiled pleasantly at Peg, ignoring Nell.

'Dearest! How are you after the birth of your baby girl? Ruperta, isn't it? I daresay the Prince thinks her the most perfect child, for Charles absolutely *adores* our own little Charles, and Stuart men are all the same, they simply adore babies!'

This was said in a careful and almost perfect English accent and Nell thought, with an inward grin, that Louise must have been rehearsing the speech as she sat on the other side of the room for usually her accent was indisputably French.

Now Nell leant forward, saying 'Very true! My own little lads could not have a more loving father than the King. I declare, he worships them. But Prince Rupert, of course, is only half a Stuart and may see his child through less rose-tinted spectacles!'

Louise turned her shoulder on Nell, continuing as if the other had not spoken, 'Have you heard how the little Italian Princess took the news that she was to wed the Duke of York? She screamed and wept for two days and nights, and vowed she would infinitely prefer the cloister!'

'And she's not met Dismal Jimmy yet, so cannot know he is as unfaithful as he is ugly,' Nell broke in, twinkling at Peg. 'But there, beauty is not everything. I suppose there are some who would say my keeper, with his long nose and dark skin, was not handsome. But...'

'How *dare* you speak of ze King in such a disrespectful manner,' Louise cried, in a voice throbbing with passion. 'He is the handsomest and best of men!'

'An admission!' Nell said triumphantly. 'Not only does she admit she heard my voice, but that the King is my keeper. Wonders will never cease!'

Louise descended abruptly from her high horse, shooting Nell a fulminating glance as she sat between the two women on the couch. 'You are so irritating, Nellee,' she said sulkily. 'How can I enjoy to admit that you are also ze – the – King's mistress? It is an admission of failure, that. By now, with my looks and breeding, I should be all that he needs.'

'There's no accounting for tastes,' Nell said serenely. 'Some men, my dear Duchess, prefer prettiness to classic beauty, and liveliness to breeding.'

'Oh, phoo,' Louise said scornfully. 'He *adores* me, and finds in me everything he can desire. You, he keeps out of ... of...'

'Yes, go on,' Nell said. She had been sitting doing a tapestry destined for the seat of one of her new chairs and the long, shining tapestry needle was held in her hand, pointing towards Louise's plump thigh, in a manner horribly suggestive of a dagger.

'Nellee, if you, if you *dare* to ... to...' Louise

began, her eyes widening. 'Such a threat would be unbelievable at any court but this! That you, a mere actress, should threaten me, a member of ze nobility—' as the needle moved she said imploringly, 'Mistress Hughes, stop her, I beg!'

'She's done nothing,' Peg said mildly. 'And you must remember that I was an actress, too. But perhaps it would be best if you were to decide that King Charles keeps Mistress Gwyn out of love and respect for her.'

Louise eyed the needle, glanced up into Nell's dancing eyes, then eyed the needle again. It remained steady as a rock, pointing at her. 'Oh, very well,' she said, conceding defeat. 'I suppose it is true that he's fond of you ... in certain ways, at any rate.'

The needle point dipped once more into the tapestry and Louise got to her feet and trotted quickly away from the sofa. Peg and Nell looked at one another and smiled. 'Round one to you today, Nell,' Peg said. 'But I wonder who will win tomorrow?'

'Me,' Nell said promptly. 'She is so aware of her rank and dignity that countless opportunities of putting me down are lost. And besides she has not the intelligence to be clever at my expense, nor I think, the quickness of wit. She just harps on about how common I am, and how vulgar, and that seems to satisfy her.'

'I must say I'm glad she doesn't dig her talons into me,' Peg said, staring over to where Louise, with many gestures, was apparently confiding in Lady Coventry how near she had come to being stuck in the leg. 'I wouldn't know how to combat it.'

'Prince Rupert would not see you humiliated,' Nell said at once. 'And you aren't common anyway, Peg. But the Prince is your protection against spite.'

'And what of the King? Will he not protect you?'

'Goodness no, he's far too easy going. He lets us fight our own battles. But he won't send me away, for all Louise's importunings, because he is fond of me.'

'Nell, do you *mind* being merely one of a ... a harem, instead of the only woman in your man's life?' Peg asked.

Nell finished her stitch, clipped the wool and began to thread a new colour. 'Yes I do, but minding will not mend matters. He cannot help his nature, poor darling. There is no man living who needs a variety of women more than Charles does. His life has been so uncertain, you see, right from the early days. I think he takes from each one of his mistresses something he needs, which he cannot find in one woman. Louise is Catholic and a lady who has become his whore through politics; Barbara is a high-born lady with the morals of a an alley cat, and the experience and appetite of one as well. And I am frankly, gloriously and unrepentantly common. I don't talk like a lady or act like a lady because I'm not a lady! I'm a little whore from the slums, who happens to love him true. And Charles knows he is common too, which is a thing I'd never dare let Louise hear me say, needle or no needle! But it's true, Peg! Look at him in Newmarket, riding his horses, chatting to the jockeys, talking to anyone who approaches him. And when he's at sea he works like a sailor and talks like a sailor and loves every minute. Yes, although Louise mocks me for it, I'm sure he loves me for my commonness.'

'Is that why you've never learned to talk like the court ladies, (though you can when you like because you're an actress first and foremost, Nellie!) and why you curse like ... like an orange girl when you're annoyed?'

Nell nodded, grinning. 'Of course! And knowing how it infuriates Louise makes it even more amusing!'

The Queen had moved to Somerset House when it became obvious to her that Louise had become her husband's mistress, so that now, when Nell visited her lover, she did so in his own magnificent apartments. In fact, because Charles did not wish her to return to the stage, she became a regular visitor at court, though she rarely spent much time in the small room which the King set aside for her use.

But she was there one rainy summer day when Peg Hughes came running to her.

'Do come, Nellie! Such sport! You simply must see this for yourself,' was all she would say, however, and Nell, greatly intrigued, followed her friend into the room where most of the court were assembled.

It had been a good year for trade. With the Dutch war ended by the Treaty of Westminster, and with parliament quiet for once, the King had actually found himself with money in hand. With his usual generosity Louise had had pearls and diamonds and some truly magnificent toilettes, Barbara had been granted large sums of money to marry off her elder daughters, and even Nell, the least self-seeking person, had been thrilled and touched by gifts of clothing for her boys and for herself, by the prettiest gold and pearl necklace, and by a supply of wine, sent to stock her cellars. So when Peg implored her to 'look at Louise', she expected to see her rival flaunting more jewellery, or finer garments.

But Louise, her face animated as she chatted to Mary of Modena, did not seem to be dressed with any particular brilliance – quite the opposite. She was clad from head to foot in funereal black.

Nell, never one to shrink from asking questions, strolled over to Louise, saying in her forthright way, 'What's all this, then? Has someone died?'

Louise swung round, glancing down from her superior height with an annoying air of consequence. 'Of *course*,' she said pettishly. 'Do you think that I would dress in black because it suited me, merely?'

'Oh, I'm sure you would, *if* it suited you,' Nell said pointedly. 'Red-heads and yellow-heads look beautiful in black, and those with really black hair, too. But women with brown hair should not wear it. Makes 'em look dowdy.'

'My 'air – hair is a veree dark brown,' Louise said coldly. 'But in any event I am in *mourning*, which is why I wear black. Not because I choose it.'

'Oh, yes? For whom?' Nell said, noticing regretfully that Louise was beginning to correct her English, for she knew how excellent a mimic Nell was, and how frequently her own broken French accent, saying ridiculous, unworthy things, could be heard around Whitehall, coming from that teasing, tilted mouth.

'For a dear friend and relation,' Louise said. 'A *French* relation, Nellee.'

'Well, I'm sorry for your loss,' Nell said handsomely, wondering why Peg had called her if it was indeed so. 'A close relative, was it? A parent, perhaps?'

'Not so close a zat – that,' Louise admitted. 'It is the Prince de Rohan, a nobleman of Louis's court, and a connection of my family.'

'Oh, I see! An *imaginary* connection,' Nell said, nodding sympathetically. 'How sad, Louise. Accept my sincere sympathy.'

She walked away, leaving Louise still trying to work out the precise meaning of 'imaginary connection', and sought Peg, working away in a corner on a white and primrose shawl for Ruperta.

Peg put her work down and raised her eyes to Nell's face, smiling broadly. 'Isn't she ridiculous, Nellie? When I saw the extent of her mourning, and knew it to be for the Prince de Rohan, who can have only the slightest relationship to Louise, if indeed any, I had to smile. It makes her appear absurd but does she see it? Not she!'

'Oh, she will,' Nell said, smiling so that her dimples peeped. 'She will see it, dear Peggy, given time!'

And sure enough, next day Nell walked amongst the court clad from head to foot in black; so swathed indeed, that but for her small stature and the unmistakable flame of her hair, she would have been unrecognisable.

Peggy, guessing what was afoot, called, 'Come over here, Nellie. The King is here and does not much admire your dress.'

Nell approached, her face showing caution, for she knew that Charles did not like her to tease Louise. But she could see the beginnings of a smile jerking the corners of his mobile mouth, and relaxed a little.

Louise, who had been sitting beside him, talking animatedly, glared at Nell, but did not speak, so that it was Charles, carefully neutral, who said, 'Nellie, my dear, why black? Surely you cannot be in mourning too? And if so, for whom?'

Nell gave vent to a great sigh, followed by a tiny, choked back sob. 'Indeed, Charles, I *am* in mourning. Have you not heard? The Cham of Tartary is dead.'

'Yes, I had heard,' Charles said, glancing down at his feet, his lips twitching. 'But I shall not give you the satisfaction of asking you why you should go into mourning for him, little one.'

'But I shall,' Louise said, her face reddening furiously. 'What *right* have you got to go into mourning for the Cham of Tartary? You have done it merely to mock me! What relative is the Cham of Tartary to you?'

The King, guessing the answer, had half raised his hand at the beginning of her speech, but he subsided with a rueful grin, seeing that Louise was determined to lay herself open to Nell's wit.

'Why, by an odd coincidence, exactly the same relation that the Prince of Rohan was to you,' Nell said, giving Louise her sweetest smile. 'And perhaps you can tell me, Duchess, how long our mourning should last?'

'And without deigning a reply, she swep' out,' Charles said, chuckling, as Louise left the room in a flurry of black taffeta. 'Well I'm grateful to you for one thing, little one. I daresay you'll both change out of your mourning now which will please me, for a couple of mistresses dressed like crows is the last thing I need.'

And the joke, which amused the court highly, had one other consequence. The Queen sent for Nell.

'You have a great sense of humour, Mistress Gwyn,' Queen Catherine said, smiling at the younger woman. 'Did you know that I've been forced to dismiss many of my Catholic women? Well, I must replace them with Protestants, of course. Would you like to become a Lady of the Bedchamber?'

'*What*, your Grace?' Nell squeaked. 'Me? *Me*? Ooh, you couldn't mean it. Think what the others would say!'

'You mean Mistress Queroalle? Or Carwell, as the English call her? My dear, I could have had her dismissed my service, and she knows it, for she is a Catholic. I kept her, because it pleased my husband and made his life a little easier. And you, I want partly for yourself, because you and I can laugh together over the Duchess Portsmouth hey?, and partly to please the King. At the moment, when he wants you to accompany the court, he has to risk scenes with Louise. She says he invites you to accompany us not because he wants you, but because it gives her pain. This worries my husband, and I will not have him worried if in any way, I can save him. He has enough to worry him, with parliament seeing Popish plots in every bush, and trying to prove the King spends money on his women and bastards which belongs elsewhere. So I may go ahead then, and have your appointment confirmed?'

'She did it to please Charles, of course,' Peg said thoughtfully, when Nell told her of her new position. 'She loves him so *very* much, Nellie! And it will please him, because he hates to be disliked, and to have his women sulk and turn cold on him is worse. But now he can say, with truth, that your presence is none of his doing.'

'Yes, that's true. It will be fun to be a Lady of the Bedchamber, of course. But oh, the happiness! Louise will be fit to kill me!'

Nell was right, but just before Christmas, something happened which brought herself and Louise into temporary alliance. Nell had been at home, visiting her boys, and had returned to Whitehall feeling content with her lot. Young Jamie and Darkie were fine, healthy little lads and she had played ball with them in the garden, pushed Jamie on his swing, and run races with Spot, the fat little spaniel pup their father had given them.

It was a cold, crisp day, with frost in the air and despite the sunshine, Nell thought there was a taste of snow in the air. So she trotted along briskly, the air whipping colour into her cheeks and polishing her nose like a cherry. She went straight through the corridors to the privy chamber where the Queen's women would be helping their mistress to dress at this time of the morning, and was about to enter the room when she heard, in the courtyard outside, the clatter and jingle of an arrival.

Could Charles have been out riding already, despite the chill of the morning? It was quite likely, particularly since it was too frosty for his much-loved game of tennis, and it would be nice to see him before Louise, and to feel his arms to go round her in that hard, exuberant hug which she knew meant he was in the best of health and spirits.

She had taken off her scarlet coat with the silver braiding but now she slung it round her shoulders again, and holding her muff casually by its strings, ran through the side door and out into the stableyard.

A curious sight met her eyes. Charles, hat in hand, his coat casually unbuttoned, was halfway across the yard and frozen, it seemed, into immobility by a small retinue of riders who were even now dismounting in the yard. At the head of them was a glorious young gallant with dark, smouldering eyes, a sensuous mouth, and an abundance of thickly curling black hair, held back from his face by a narrow ribbon tied at the nape of his neck. He wore a tall hat, but he doffed it now, scratching his head idly and calling, 'Hi, Frankie, come and take this confounded whip, will you?'

He spoke English but with a foreign accent and even as Nell stared, he handed his whip to a little black pageboy and swung himself gracefully down from his mount. As he turned he caught sight of the King, and stopped short.

'Charles?' he said uncertainly. 'It is Charles, isn't it?'

His voice, light as it was, seemed to tremble on the question, and Nell, staring, saw Charles suddenly throw his head back and give a roar of laughter, and then come across and hug the young man, who hugged him back without demur.

'My God, if it isn't Hortense Mazarin!' Charles said, still smiling. 'What is this all about, my dear? You're a married woman and should not be gallivanting across England in men's breeches and without your husband! It simply isn't done, my girl. What *would* your uncle, the Cardinal, say?'

Nell gasped. It was a woman! One of those Mazarin nieces who were reputed both to be great beauties and great courtesans. It was obvious from the way she had greeted the King that she had come to court for one purpose and one purpose only. Equally obviously, Charles would be only too delighted to add such a beautiful and daring mistress to his harem. And judging from what she had seen of the woman, Nell did not doubt that she was far from cold.

As they moved towards the side door. Nell turned to flee but Charles had already seen her. 'Hi Nellie, I want to introduce you to an old friend of mine,' he called. 'Don't say I must call my Nellie shy?'

Nell, turning back reluctantly, said, 'Shy? Why, no. But even I would think twice before cantering across London astride a great horse, dressed as a man!'

'But surely, dear madam, there could be fewer safer ways to travel?' Hortense's dark eyes gazed seriously at Nell. 'I have half-a-dozen retainers only and no couch or carrying chair. Since I am on horseback, why not use the safety of male costume, for few would stop a stripling for whatever money he might have in his purse, whereas a woman...'

Nell looked at the other woman's beautiful face and smiled suddenly.

'I concede your good sense then, Mistress Mazarin. And now, Charles, shall I take your, er, friend to the Stone gallery, so that you may meet her officially?' She turned to Hortense. 'Perhaps it might be better if you changed into a gown, because the Queen will be present. If your luggage has not yet arrived then we might procure one for you, from somewhere.'

Charles, adept at reading Nell's thoughts, said warningly, 'Nellie, if you lend Hortense a gown of your own, and she a full foot taller than you, I'll ... I'll...'

'As if I would,' Nell said, turning her reproachful gaze on him. 'We will prevail upon the Lady Arabella Churchill to lend one of her gowns. She and this lady are much of a height.' She took Hortense's arm. 'Come with me, my dear ... Hortense, is it? Why, you are well-named indeed! I've a mind to call you something a little less formal, though. My name is Eleanor, but I am called Nell. And I suppose one could call you "Horty", or better still, "Hor ..."'

'Nellie!' Charles said, his voice breaking on a laugh. 'I warn you, you little devil, that if you want a good hiding, you will continue in this vein. I'll not have my visitors teased or insulted by you.'

'Remember you can't forbid me the court, for I'm one of the Queen's ladies,' Nell reminded him demurely. 'But for you, Charles, just for you, I'll be good.'

And she was good. Despite the fact that in Arabella's best gown of white and rose tiffany Hortense looked ravishing, Nell continued to be genuinely kind to the other woman and to introduce her to other members of the court.

James, Duke of Monmouth, who alternately scorned and courted Nell according to his humour, came to her home that first evening to congratulate her on her acceptance of another rival in Charles's affections.

'Well, it annoys Louise, which is fun,' Nell said frankly, sitting down on her gold satin sofa and patting the seat beside her. 'Do sit down, Monmouth, don't loom over me! You should have seen poor Louise's face when she first clapped eyes on Horty! She's been letting herself go a bit, has Louise. Portly Portsmouth, she should be called! She was reclining on a low couch, eating sugar plums in a white frilly gown which made her look twice the size, and she just stopped, with a plum halfway to her mouth and stared. And then Charles, wicked devil that he is, made her get up to be presented to Hortense, and it was all she could do to heave herself off the sofa. And Charles stood there, with his hand lightly resting on Hortense's nicely curved hip, and made some drawling remark about the penalties of never exercising, not even in bed! Poor Louise went redder than a turkey cock, for she likes to be thought of as an energetic performer in *that* field, if no other. But I was glad I've kept my figure, or she would have shown me up, too.'

'I'll say this, Nellie. I've never liked Louise above half, but my father knew what he was about when he took you,' Monmouth said. He patted her thigh. 'And Hortense – God, her reputation alone tells you what she must be like in bed! Scarcely a nobleman in

Europe but has enjoyed her!' He frowned, gripping his hands into fists. 'I love a long-legged, deep-breasted woman! But my father will have her for all he's forty-five years old and should be long past such things. The rest of us won't stand a chance.'

'He's got such a way with him,' Nell said. 'But why you should talk so I can't imagine, for you are just such another and will be the same at forty-five, if you live that long! You're a born troublemaker, Mon, but in other respects you're just like your father and your uncle. Charles enjoys women and shows it, Dismal Jimmy enjoys women but thinks it a penance, and you enjoy other people's women, because it adds spice to the dish.'

'Women are meant to be enjoyed, especially by the young,' Monmouth said, putting his arm round Nell and trying to turn her to face him. 'Come on, Nell, be kind to me! Hortense is too old for me anyway!'

'Stop that,' Nell said sharply, pushing him off the sofa. 'I'm your friend, Mon, whilst you love your father and treat him as a good son should. And no good son hunts his father's women, just remember that. What do you mean, anyway, that Hortense is too old for you? She's twenty, or so she said.'

'Twenty? Use your head, Nell,' Monmouth said, sitting down on the couch again and apparently not at all annoyed by her sharp rebuff. 'She's thirty if she's a day. She was suggested as a bride for my father before he came to the throne. But she's got the sort of dark Latin good looks which stay young for years and then age overnight.'

'Then pray heaven night will soon fall,' Nell said devoutly. 'The Queen, poor dear, takes it in her stride, but this is the first time Louise has had her nose put out of joint. I wonder how she'll take it?'

'Badly,' Monmouth prophesied. 'She thinks she's chief whore at court and that makes up for having to be a whore at all. And now she'll find she's second whore and she won't like it.'

'She's always been second whore,' Nell said indignantly. 'I don't count Barbara because she was out of it, really, before Louise came along. But I was first in Charles's bed and first in his affections, too. I may have to give best to this Italian adventuress but I shan't do it willingly, or without a fight. I've noticed, Mon, that whenever your father's interest lights on someone new my wine bill goes longer before it's paid, and the boys's stockings grow more threadbare before being replaced.'

'You should be more demanding. Father would shell out sooner than be nagged,' Monmouth observed sagely. 'You should ask, Nellie, for the boys's sake.'

'Well, since she's been whoring round Europe for ten years I suppose at least she won't condescend to me! Oh, and that reminds me. Who is Barbara bedding now?'

Monmouth, who had stood up to leave, lingered for a moment, his handsome, sulky face suddenly made charming by his smile. 'Haven't you heard, Nellie? The King caught her in bed with John Churchill, Arabella's brother. Poor John climbed out of the window with nothing on but his socks!'

They stood in the doorway, chuckling, until Nell said, 'But John is a mere boy, Mon, and Barbara is ... well, she's ageing rapidly and getting so fat, and...'

'She pays him,' Monmouth said briefly, the laughter fading from his eyes and his mouth showing his distaste. 'By God, but I'd ask a fortune before I'd bed Barbara now.'

He raised his hand in mocking salute and left her and Nell turned thoughtfully back into the house. One day, she reminded herself, I shall be old. One day I may even be fat if I don't take care. And I've never pestered Charles for money, or titles, or property. All I've got is this house, and all the boys have got is me and their father. She remembered Monmouth's mouth when he'd spoken of bedding Barbara. How dreadful to have to force oneself on a man, not for the sake of pleasuring oneself, but for sheer financial necessity! Slowly climbing the stairs, she thought what would I do, if Charles were to die tomorrow? No, not tomorrow, because now I could still earn my living on the stage. But what if he were to die in twenty years – in ten? How could she run the house, pay the bills? Charles had never given her money and she had never asked for any.

I could sell my jewels and my plate, she thought, picking up the candle which Lucy had left out for her and making her way towards her bedchamber. But how long would that keep us. A year? Six months? And what then?

Far into the night she wrestled with the problem but found no solution, and finally fell asleep knowing that for the boys' sake, she must begin to make provision for a future without her lover.

# Eleven

'Peggy! Come in, and tell me how you've been keeping. What are you doing at Windsor? Or have you just come because of the King's illness?'

Peg walked across the soft blues of the carpet, glancing with approval at the lemon and white hangings, the bowl of pink and red roses on the low, highly polished table, the china cupids on the mantel. 'It's good to see you again, Nellie,' she said. 'And it is sad that it had taken the King's illness to bring us together again, but you know how it is. The house in Hammersmith is large, and needs my constant attention, as does my daughter, little monkey that she is! But we are here constantly too, because Rupert is Governor of Windsor Castle, yet we seem to have missed each other this year.'

'Well, we're together now,' Nell said,

231

gesturing to a chair. 'Sit down, Peg, and tell me how you like my new house!'

'Nice,' Peg said approvingly. 'Is it let, or lent, or what?'

'It's mine, from Charles,' Nell said. 'I'm glad you like it. Charles and I had a thoroughly enjoyable time fitting it out and buying furniture and carpets. Now, have you been to the castle? Charles is much better now, for last week the physicians despaired of his life, you know.'

'Yes, I've seen the King. He certainly seemed well and cheerful. But what a time he has lived through, no wonder he nearly died! All the plottings started by that wretched creature, Titus Oates, which have led to the worst persecution of Catholics since the time of Cromwell, I should think. His position must have been intolerable, with his brother and his wife both Catholics.'

'Charles behaved wonderfully,' Nell said. 'They wanted the Queen's life, you know. Poor little Catherine, whose only crime is that of loving her husband and abiding by the laws of his country! He sent James away, of course. It was the wisest thing to do, and

Dismal Jimmy is so tactless, Peggy, that he would make trouble for the archangel Gabriel himself. But the King stuck to his guns, no matter what. He said when the whole business began to grow out of all proportion that he would abide by the decision of the judges, that law in England was law, and must be upheld. And he did it, and we are just, but only just, beginning to see the light at the end of the tunnel.'

'And Monmouth?'

'He knows that he is the Protestant hope; he knows that his best chance of the crown will be through the people's refusing to be ruled by a Catholic monarch. Charles is gentle with him, but I think he is wrong. Monmouth has been spoilt all his life and it's about time he was made to realise he is being used as a pawn by these people, not because of any intrinsic value in himself.'

'That's a bit harsh, isn't it, Nellie? I thought you quite liked the boy.'

'Not when he worries Charles I don't. But let's talk of something else, Peg. This persecution business has been terrible, but pray God it is ending at last.'

'All right. I meant to ask you when I first

came in, who is the lady, picking roses in the garden? She smiled at me and I thought I'd seen her somewhere before, but couldn't place her.'

'Oh, that was Rose. My sister, you know. She was widowed recently, but Charles pays her a pension, and when she heard of his illness she came down to Windsor at once. She lives in the country now and I don't see much of her, so she wanted to speak to me about my mother's death. She came up to London for the funeral but had to go back to her children the same day, so now she has left them with a nurse, and is having a little holiday.'

'I didn't know your mother was dead. I'm so sorry, Nell. Did she die at your house in Pall Mall, or down here?'

'She died in her own place, a cottage in Chelsea by the river. Or actually, she died outside it. To be blunt, she was drowned, and probably fell into the water after drinking a bottle of brandy. The thing was, Peg, that I'd found it impossible to live in the same house with her. She was drinking more and more heavily, she was dirty and wouldn't wash, and some of her habits ...

Well, it doesn't bear thinking about. So I found her a capable servant, and a man to run her errands and keep in touch with me, and set her up in Chelsea. She seemed happy there, and I thought it better all round. And then one day the servant came to see me, very distressed. Ma took herself outside, one bright afternoon, as she did often, to watch the river traffic. There was a wooden seat by the river and she liked to sit on that and watch the world go by. But on this particular afternoon, she must have been accompanied by a bottle of brandy, unbeknown to the servant. When the woman went to call Ma in to her dinner she found the seat overturned, an empty brandy bottle beneath it, and Ma floating face downwards in the river.'

'I see,' Peg said, a little taken aback by Nell's frankness. 'Now Nellie, one reason I've come calling this afternoon is because Rupert and I have been discussing you, and we're worried.'

Nell did not reply, merely raising her eyebrows enquiringly.

'God knows, my dear, that Charles has had mistresses in plenty,' Peg said bluntly.

'And one way and another they've all feathered their nests with whatever he can afford to give them. But you have been different. You live in a house which he's given you and he pays your bills. But what else have you and the boys? What would happen to you if the King died tomorrow? You would have no *money*, my dear. You'd have to sell both houses, and try to earn a living in some fashion. We're worried for your sake, Nellie, and for the boys.'

'I know, I know,' Nell said sombrely. 'I realised my position some while ago, when Hortense first came to England. I saw that without Charles I would be nothing and the boys nobodies. I stood in my bedchamber that night and vowed that I would make a place for myself and for my sons so that when Charles died, we would have something left. And I've made a start, Peggy. The elder, Darkie, is Baron of Headington and Earl of Burford, and Jamie is being educated in Paris, at the King's expense. He's made him Lord Bronckton. Even his pocket money is paid for by Charles so I've no worries there. And though I *cannot* bring myself to ask for money when I know he is so hard up, I am more careful than I was. Some of his gifts are not fit for me, some of the jewellery is too grand, and that is earmarked for sale if something were to occur, and the proceeds would go to the boys.'

'Baron of Headington and Earl of Burford sounds very well,' Peg said. 'But what land, what money goes with them? They are empty titles, Nell, and you *must* press for something more! Take heed from Charles's illness, which might easily have proved fatal. You are a young woman, in your middle twenties, with many years ahead of you. I know that you hate to nag, and that you've a generous disposition. But for your sons' sake...'

'What else can I do?' Nell asked. 'There are so many bastards to provide for, Peg! The King does his best for this one and that one, but for myself, it is *he* who is important. And the boys of course. My sons.'

'Well, for a start, don't antagonise Monmouth,' Peg said firmly. 'I know he's an unpleasant young man in many ways, and that he gives Charles more trouble than pleasure at the moment. But the people cheer for him and call him the Protestant Duke, and they mutter at York and call him the Catholic Duke. If Monmouth *should* come to the throne...'

'Charles would never see Dismal Jimmy pushed out, not even for his adored eldest,' Nell protested. 'And if you've been told that I called him 'Prince Perkin' at a supper party, then I can only tell you he was being intolerable! He called me a miserable little whore, and I told him I was no more whore than Lucy Barlow, and only miserable because he was present. Everyone laughed, I can tell you.'

'So I heard,' Peg said dryly. 'But can you not see, Nell, that there is a great deal of feeling for Monmouth in the country? They want a Protestant King to follow Charles, and they're afraid of James, and the Pope. You must not antagonise him, because if he gets the crown he'll remember, and see that you and the boys suffer for it.'

'He'll never get the crown,' Nell said with conviction. 'But I see what you mean, Peg, and I thank you. I will try and cultivate him, and the truth is, I could like the fellow if he were not to work against his father. He makes it difficult for Charles to love him, although Charles cannot help but love him, despite himself. But he's gone too far this time, with his deliberate stirrings up of the anti-Catholic faction. Charles has said several times how peaceful it is with James safely in Brussels, and last time Monmouth was difficult Charles said that for his own good, his son might be sent to Holland for a few months. He's said it before of course, but this time I think he means it.'

'That's possible,' Peg said, getting to her feet. 'I must go now, Nell, for Rupert is at Windsor and will be wondering where I am. I'd not realised you'd your own house here now, and had expected to find you in apartments at the castle.'

'I'd walk back with you if I could,' Nell said wistfully. 'For towards evening Charles loves to fish, and I love to sit quietly beside him, watching. But Rose has come down especially to see me, so I cannot go out and leave her here alone.'

'Oh, that reminds me of the second reason I wanted to see you,' Peg said, turning in the doorway. 'I am having a small supper party in my rooms at Windsor tonight. Louise will be there, and Hortense, and many of our friends. Would you and your sister care to join us? If *you* are there, Nellie, the King is sure to come.'

'Oh thank you, that would be delightful,' Nell said, brightening. 'Did you know they've summoned the Duke of York home, by the way? Just because of the King's illness of course. He is, after all, the heir, and if things had gone badly for Charles ... But anyway, is he at Windsor yet?'

'Not yet, I think,' Peg told her. 'But come over, Nellie and bring your sister, if she would like to come.'

Despite the optimism of that visit to Windsor, however, the alarms and excursions of the Catholic plots and the wild imaginings of parliament continued to trouble both King and country. But Charles, as he had said, rode out the storm by simply trusting to the law and the eventual sanity of the English people. Shaftesbury, who wanted to see Charles out and a republic in, left no stone unturned to trouble the King. He packed juries so that only his own men would get favourable verdicts, he raised private armies to harry the honest few who stood by law and order, he stirred up the London apprentices, never a difficult task. But Charles wore him down.

And peace came slowly back with the autumn, so that once more they were at Windsor, enjoying a quiet evening's fishing, when they heard that Shaftesbury had given up, had realised that he would not, this time, be able to bully or browbeat his way out of the trouble he was in, and had fled to Holland.

'And where is Monmouth, sir?' asked Nell, watching the float bob on the water.

'In hiding, the silly young fool,' Charles said lazily. 'He may have gone back to Holland again, for the matter of that. At any rate, he's not bothering me at present. Nor upsetting the country.'

Across the grass from the castle a messenger in the King's livery came trotting towards them, a roll of parchment in his hand.

A discreet cough and he handed the message over, then jog-trotted back to the castle. Charles sat down again on the grass beside Nell, and handed her his rod. 'Hold it carefully, don't dip the end too much,' he instructed her. 'I don't suppose you'll get a bite, it's getting chilly and we should pack up now, but I'd better read this before we move on.'

She was becoming a restful companion he reflected, as he tore open the seal. Her liveliness was infectious in company, and her merry laugh, her quick wit, could always keep him amused. But when they were alone her undemanding presence and her love for him were totally restful, so that he wanted her with him, and was conscious of missing her presence when she was in her own home.

He glanced down at her. The sweep of autumn coloured hair, the creamy pallor of her skin, the bright, sherry coloured eyes. She looked like a beautiful child; could she really be the mother of those two hefty lads, Charles and Jamie Beauclerk? He glanced down at the despatch. Ah, it came from Paris so there might be news of Jamie. She would be doubly interested, for she adored her boys.

He began to read the first letter, and felt his heart sink like a stone. He heard himelf groan, and turned back to re-read the words even as Nell turned to him, her face expressing her anxious love.

'What is it now, Charles? Oh my darling, how dare they worry you here, when you need so badly to be quiet, and at peace.'

He found he could not answer her for the lump in his throat, but his arm went out and hugged her to him, whilst hot tears formed in his eyes.

'What *is* it?' she was asking, fear in her voice. 'My poor darling, what is it?'

And then, from somewhere, he found the courage to tell her. James Beauclerk, Lord Bronckton, not yet nine years old, had died in Paris.

# **Twelve**

'Well, Louise, we've seen Newmarket many times, over the years. But this year we're seeing it not as a refuge from the troubles of London, but as a town we love. Because truly, peace seems to have come to the capital as well as to the rest of England. Wonderful, not to have Shaftesbury and his wretched followers – the Faction, Charles calls them – snarling and worrying round the King's every move. Do you love Newmarket? It makes me feel so calm and good, and happy, too.'

'We all love Newmarket, because Charles does. It is a friendly place, and as you say, a refuge from court. Oh, I know court is no longer the frightening place it has been these past two or three years, but even so, we can all behave with a lack of dignity here! Even Hortense, who is a city creature, is content.'

Louise and Nell, sitting on two of the fattest and placidest ponies the King could procure, were ambling home after a tiring but enjoyable day spent watching the races, riding around the quiet, flat countryside, and finally in ambling home as the sun was sinking in the sky.

Nell, looking with affection at her old rival, saw how time had mellowed them both. Louise was unashamedly plump now, but though her air of childish innocence had gone Nell thought her kinder and better than she had been when young, for now her affection for Charles was real, as her friendship for Nell herself was genuine. Once, she had loved Charles only because he was the King, but Charles's own truth and honesty had won her heart, so that she loved him for himself.

'Have I changed much, Louise?' Nell asked, twisting round on her pony's back so that she could see the other's face. 'Not just in looks, but in character?'

'Oh yes,' Louise said instantly. 'You are much gentler, Nellee, much softer! But your figure and face have not changed even a little bit! You have a spring in your step and a lightness in you which I cannot think will ever change! Why do you ask?'

'Because, I suppose, we are all here, now. All the old crowd! James has returned and is actually popular with the people, and is cheered when he rides through the streets. Our sons are with us, Barbara is back at court for a while, the Queen and her little priests no longer fear the mob when they appear in public. Only poor Peg is missing.'

Rupert had died six months before and Peg mourned him still – would mourn him, Nell knew, for always. She had sold Nell the magnificent pearls Rupert had given her, for 'I shan't want them now since I don't intend to come to court,' she told her friend. 'I only came to Whitehall for Rupert's sake, and now I shall stay quietly at home for my own.'

'And Monmouth,' Louise reminded her now, with a spark of the old, jealous look. 'He's not here, and I'm thankful for it. Better that he should be in exile than here, working to do Charles hurt.'

'Oh, he isn't so bad,' Nell protested un-easily. 'The King misses him so sadly, Louise, that I could almost wish him back for his sake! And the Queen loves him too. Though she's not so very much older than him really.'

'Well, I don't,' Louise said. 'He is evil, Nellee! How you can stand up for him after the things he's said about you ... But there, he isn't here, we must be grateful for the peace his absence brings.'

They rode into the town then, and fore-gathered in the coffee room of the inn where Charles was staying. And after they had watched a play, enacted in the inn yard, and supped quietly, they made their way to their respective rooms.

Nell was in bed, and snuggling under the covers, for it was a cool night, with a brisk wind blowing, when there was a scratching on her door and Charles entered. 'I can't sleep alone,' he complained as Nell moved over to make way for him. 'I need someone warm and cuddly on a night like this. Hear that wind, little one?'

They lay for a little, not making love but talking quietly of past good times, of race meetings and cock fights and theatre trips.

They were ready for sleep, curled up and cosy, when a commotion outside brought

Charles bounding out of bed. Peering through the shutters, he exclaimed, 'Fire! There are boys running down the street, calling fire. Get up, Nellie!'

But she was already out of bed, standing in the window dragging on her clothes, whilst she watched, with awe and horror, Newmarket burning.

'Do you mean to tell me, Nell, that the flight from Newmarket, a week earlier than you had meant to leave, was truly the result of *chance*? That had not a careless groom knocked out his pipe too near some bales of straw the court would have left the town at the end of March, as they had planned?'

Nell, still shocked herself at the recent discovery of the plot to kill the King and the Duke of York, which had misfired merely because of the change of plan at Newmarket, nodded.

'Then it was *chance* which saved the King and the Duke from being waylaid and killed by the Rye House conspirators, and not some prior warning? Dear God, on what a slender thread hangs fate! And Monmouth, presumably, would have been made King?

Oh, Nellie, how would England have stood, then? And what has Charles done to deserve such a son?'

Nell said quickly, only half-believing it herself, 'He knew of no plot to *kill* Charles or James, Rosie! Or so he maintains, and I *have* to believe him, for Charles does. He says he knows Monmouth meant him no actual harm, but oh, Rose, the pain in his eyes! Sometimes I cannot bear it.'

'And what will happen? They've caught the conspirators, so will they deal with them as they should, or will they be allowed to go away, and sin again?'

The two sisters were in Nell's summer garden, sitting on cushioned chairs amongst the lavender bushes, for Rose was newly married to Captain Forster, and had come up for a short visit to London from her country home, all agog to hear about the Rye House conspiracy which was causing such a stir in the country.

'They've caught most of them, and this time they will be judged, and punished. Not Monmouth, though. He fled to Holland and Charles says he was a pawn in the hands of unscrupulous men. And that is *true*, Rose, even if he did know the King was to die. It takes all Charles's experience and intelligence and political tact to hold the country together and govern it for its own good, and the people love him. How much statecraft do you suppose Monmouth has? Or would be allowed to use, for that matter? The men who push him forward are power-hungry for themselves; he is merely a good figurehead to oppose James. Or, it seems, to oppose his own father! Charles says that this time, he won't raise a finger to stop the law taking its course. But he was terribly moved and distressed when they told him Essex had cut his throat, in prison. He said, 'My Lord of Essex need not have despaired of mercy, for I owe him a life.' But it would have been difficult to save him, and see the others suffer. Essex's father, you know, died on the scaffold for Charles's father.'

'No, I didn't know,' Rose said. 'But how could Monmouth, who knows the King so well, do such a thing? Will he come home and beg his father's pardon?'

'It is being discussed,' Nell said cautiously. 'But we're off in a few days, first to Windsor and then to Winchester, from there to

Portsmouth and Southampton – it does us good to get out of the capital, where such dreadful things have happened, or at least, were planned to happen.'

Sure enough, Monmouth did return to court, to beg his father's forgiveness and to sign a confession of his part in the plot in return for a promise that he should not suffer for it.

Nell saw with pleasure how her lover's face brightened, how light his step became, when he had that beloved, treacherous eldest son safe by his side once more. But his pleasure was shortlived. Back in England, Monmouth quickly fell under the influence of those fatal friends who had beguiled him into the Rye House plot. They told him that if he was to be forgiven, then he should stand up and say the Plot was a nonsense, dreamed up by the King and the Duke to punish those innocent subjects who chose to stand against him in parliament. And two of them, Trenchard and Hampden, so worked upon his weak and vacillating nature that they managed to convince him that his signed confession would hang them, and do the Faction untold harm.

Despite his father's sworn word – which had never been broken yet – that he should never be called upon to give evidence, that the prisoners in the Tower should be bailed, and that no-one would suffer as a result of his confession, Monmouth went to White-hall and asked for his declaration back. Charles, in a fury of hurt that his son could so distrust him, after all the love and faith he had shown towards the sinner, hurled the parchment at him and told him to go to hell and to keep away from England. Mon-mouth fled again to Holland, leaving Char-les a little older, a little more tired, and with a little less will to fight his increasing ill-health.

But Nell, to her pleasure, still managed to cheer the King however low his spirits might become. Dancing up to him one day during the extreme cold of that winter, bright as a berry in her scarlet coat and cap with her hands in a great ermine muff, she offered to teach him to skate on the frozen Thames, where citizens were making bonfires, watch-ing sports, indulging in coach races, and roasting oxen.

Charles, watching from the bank, said doubtfully, 'I used to skate, years ago. There is that cursed pain in my side though. But I've not felt it today. I wonder if I might! How good are you, Nellie?'

'I expect I shall be very good,' Nell said confidently. 'I've never actually tried, but I've got natural balance, you know, and I'll keep you safe.'

'What a good thing I didn't take you seriously,' Charles said an hour later, when he was helping her off her bottom for the dozenth time. 'Natural balance, indeed! I admit you've got courage, little one, but you must be black and blue from your falls. Indeed, if I'd trusted in you to keep me upright, the folk would have been treated to the sight of the King and his mistress flat on their backs in no time at all.'

Nell giggled. 'Do you remember that first time, when I said I wouldn't lie flat on my back in the grass for you in January? Oh, Charles, but we've had some delightful times! And though I admit skating is difficult, you are marvellous at it, and made me feel as though I could skate too, when we glided round so merrily. You skate like a man half your age. Oh, look, chestnuts! Do you want some?'

He agreed and Nell hailed her son, who was skating nearby, and sent him off to purchase some nuts from the vendor, far out on the ice.

'He skates well, doesn't he? And isn't he tall and handsome in that nice new coat and hat?' Nell said, and Charles replied, 'Takes after me, I'm glad to say. I wouldn't want to have an undersized little shrimp for a son!' He glanced down at her with a teasing smile, but his eyes were tender. 'Did you know old St Albans had died?'

'No, I didn't. Did you know that Charles Hart was dead? And John Lacy?'

He looked surprised, for Hart had been younger than he by ten years, but he persisted. 'Yes, but Nell, St Albans didn't have a son to carry on the title.'

'Oh, poor old fellow,' Nell said absently. 'Here comes Darkie, with our chestnuts. I shall put mine in my muff.'

'Here comes the Duke of St Albans, with our chestnuts,' Charles corrected her gently.

'No, it is Darkie,' Nell insisted, peering into the fading afternoon. 'I would know that mop of hair anywhere. Oh!' She broke off, staring up at him, her eyes widening. 'Oh Charles! Thank you, my darling, thank you!'

She threw her arms round his neck, making him stoop to kiss her in front of all the interested, friendly passersby.

'And he will also be Registrar of the High Court of Chancery and Master Falconer of England. Fancy, Nellie, what recompense for a handful of hot chestnuts!'

She hugged him, her face brilliant with excitement. 'I don't know what a Regi-whatsit is, nor a Falconer of England, but I'll be bound it's important, and he'll get some income out of it,' she said frankly. 'Charles, you are so good to us!'

'Not nearly good enough,' he said ruefully, remembering the honours and money heaped on Barbara's children and on Louise's precious only son. 'But you've got more of my heart than any other woman ever had, little one, save for Minette.'

Darkie, skating towards them with a brown paper twist full of hot chestnuts, thought they made an attractive picture, standing on the crisp, yellowed snow at the edge of the ice in their colourful clothes, their arms round each other, their faces glowing. He handed over his burden and added his thanks to his mother's when the King told him of his new titles. But it meant more to him to see how his father loved him, and to know that his mother's glow of pleasure was, in part, due to himself.

After such a winter, the summer was almost too hot. Charles had arranged to betroth Nell's son to the rich daughter of the de Vere family but though this pleased Nell in one way it frightened her in another. It made her think that Charles was setting his life to rights, making provision for his children, because he might not be able, in a year or two, to do such things himself. She saw something in his eyes which had never been there before; a resignation, almost, and he took a pleasure in the small things of life so that every moment was cherished, every dew drop on every rose petal giving him, not only its beauty, but a memory to hold, should he not see other roses, other late and langorous summers.

He is growing old, she told herself sadly,

but are not we all? His beautiful palace at Winchester was growing, and he loved to visit it but when Wren, the architect, told him it would not be completed for a year, he showed a rare sign of impatience. 'A year is a long time,' Nell heard him murmur. 'Too long.'

Once, Nell thought, as she gazed out of her window at the new London which had sprung up from the ashes of that long-ago fire, Louise, Barbara and myself were rivals for his love. Even Hortense, that Johnny-come-lately, had been a rival, in a sense, though Nell knew now that Charles had enjoyed her company and her body, but had never given her more than the lightest affection. Yet now, when he was ageing and could have been forgiven for hoarding his love for himself and, perhaps, his children, he spread the cloak of it over all of them so that there was not one of his mistresses but felt he loved her best.

He loves his children terribly, especially that wretch, Monmouth, her thoughts ran. But his love for his people, who have treated him so badly in the past, transcends everything. And is most difficult for me to understand, though I've known him now for twenty years.

And she thought about the women who loved him, his mistresses and his Queen, watching him closely, anticipating his every wish, leaving no stone unturned to give him pleasure, save him pain. And in harmony with each other they moved through that hot, breathless summer, and into winter.

# Thirteen

'He is not dead then, Louise?'

Louise shook her head, her face ugly and swollen with weeping. 'No, not yet,' she said, through quivering lips. 'Oh, Nellee, many times he has returned to us from serious illness, yet not this time, the doctors say.'

'And we may not see him, of course?'

'Of course not. His sons may go in, later, but there is no room at such a time for you and I.'

The small ante-chamber where the King's four mistresses had gathered was hushed, as they listened for some sound from the next room. The women sat quietly, glad of each other's company during this dreadful wait. Barbara, Duchess of Cleveland, who had taken from him avidly and been unfaithful, sat trying to turn a diamond ring upon her finger. The flesh was so swollen than it would not move. She would have to have it cut off when ... She stared round her at the other faces.

'When it is over, I shall go abroad again,' she said half-defiantly. 'There is nothing for me, here, once he is dead.'

Louise nodded. 'I've only just returned from France, but I shall go back. The Duke of York is a good man, and of my faith, but it is Charles who has kept me in England all these years,' she said, and slow tears ran down her puffed, pretty cheeks and into the lace of her collar.

'I shall not return to Italy, but I shall go abroad,' Hortense agreed. 'I could not *stand* England without Charles to cheer me.'

Only Nellie did not speak of what would happen afterwards, but had she done so, she might have pointed out that of the four of them, only she would be all but destitute, once Charles was dead. And desolate, she told herself sadly.

Presently, Louise roused herself sufficiently to tell Nell that Charles had risen as usual that morning, but that he had seemed strange and unlike himself, and had suffered a seizure whilst settling down for shaving in the barber's chair. They had got him to bed, she said, but they could not leave him half-conscious as he was, and were trying to rouse him.

'Is it the end, then?' Nell asked, hardly daring to hope. 'Might it not be ... well, a seizure such as he's had before?'

Louise said gently, 'No, Nellee, he is more ill than ever before. The Queen saw me half an hour ago, and she was weeping. She said, 'This is the end, Louise; I can tell.' And she would not say that unless she believed it to be true.'

'She will go home too, to Portugal,' Nell said slowly. 'How strange it will be, without you.'

Nell waited, without weeping, pale and cold, until dusk was falling. Then she said hesitantly, 'We must eat, and I must tell Darkie to hold himself in readiness in case he is called. I will return before night.'

When she came quietly back into the room an hour later, it was to the joyful news that the King seemed a little better. He had recovered consciousness and had spoken to some of his attendants. They sat out the night, and another day. Nell went and talked to Darkie, who sat with his half-brothers, playing cards. They had seen the King for a moment, but their faces were withdrawn and sad, and they said very little.

When she would have rejoined the other women in the ante-chamber, however, she was waylaid by Louise who slipped out of the door, and caught her arm.

'Don't go in there yet, Nellee,' she said urgently. 'I have to talk to you. Will you not come to my room?'

They went together to Louise's beautiful apartment, with its silken wall-hangings and thick carpets, to find that a fire had been kindled and supper stood on a small table, close to the hearth.

'Nellee, can you fetch Barillon to me?' Louise said urgently. 'I must get a message in to the Duke of York. He has never liked me, but he knows I love the King and will listen to me, if only I can get to old Barillon.'

'What sort of a message?' Nell asked. 'Are you worrying about leaving England, Louise? The Duke isn't a bad man, he'd never stop you.'

'Oh, you mean because he's closed the ports,' Louise said, smiling for the first time that day. 'That is to keep Monmouth *out*, not to keep anyone in! But I want to see the Duke over a religious matter – or at least, Barillon. Could you do this for me?'

'Why can you not go down yourself, Louise?' Nell asked. 'Not that I mind, but why me?'

'Because you are popular, Nellee, even with the Queen and the King's ministers. They think me foreign – which is true – and conceited, which is not. They would not help me as willingly as they would help you. Will you go?'

Nell nodded and left the room at once, running to where she knew she would find Darkie, still waiting. He was curled up, half-asleep before the fire, but he woke at her touch and agreed to fetch the French ambassador. Barillon came at once, seeming unsurprised at her request, though she had seldom done more than exchange greetings with the man before.

They returned to Louise's room together, and Nell found out what the religious matter was.

'Ever since Minette made her first attempt to convert Charles to Catholicism, I believe he has wanted to be of our faith,' Louise said urgently to Barillon. 'They say he will not receive the last rites of the Protestant communion. Dear Barillon, there can only be one reason for that. I pray you, ask the Duke to see if Charles would not rather see a priest. It can hurt no-one, but could help him immeasurably. Please, Barillon.'

Nell listened, at first with astonishment but then with a growing conviction that Louise was right. He had said to her – how long ago it seemed – that night when they had discussed the difficulties of understanding the English, that English Catholics were *good*. And he had asked whether she would fear him if he were to declare to her that he was a Catholic. She knew the Catholic gentry had saved his life at the risk of their own, during the civil war. She knew how slowly and carefully, with such a long and loving memory, he had been paying, not only his own debts, but those of his father also. Tiny debts some of them, but they had not been forgotten or disregarded. No-one would be the poorer for giving him help, though it had taken him all his life to do it.

It would be like him to pay not only his material debts, but his spiritual ones too. The Catholics had saved him, yet he had not openly become one of them, for to do so would have been to bring his country to ruin and civil war once more. And now, when his country was almost in other hands, he could afford to pay this last debt.

She heard Louise sigh with relief as Barillon pattered off down the stairs again, and turned, to grasp the other's hands. 'You were right, Louise. I'm sure it is what he longs for,' she said. 'Now he can die content.' Nell and Darkie got back to the house when dawn was breaking on that last day of the King's life. Lucy, who had been dozing in front of the fire, feeding it from time to time so that it would still give out its warmth when her mistress returned, sat up with a start as the door opened.

'The King is dead, Lucy,' Nell said gently, and saw the girl run from the room in tears, her face ashen.

'So it will be everywhere,' she said dully to her son, sinking into a warmed chair and

motioning him to the other. 'But he's suffered such agony without one complaint. They
kept at him and at him, trying to revive him,
when all he wanted to do was to die. And
now he's dead, and at peace. And I have a ...
a river of tears for him, yet none of them will
fall.'

'So have I,' Darkie said, his gruff, fifteen-
year-old voice breaking on the words. 'Oh,
mother, so have I.'

He stared into the fire for a moment and
then ducked his head into his hands and she
heard the hard, tearing sobs begin, and felt
the comfort of grief as her own tears spilled
from her tired eyes.

Much later, they had some food and sat on
in the firelight, discussing their future.

'I've a heap of debts,' Nell said slowly. 'I
shall sell my jewels, of course, and my plate,
to pay them off. We'll make do somehow,
but life won't be easy for us with your father
gone.'

'What of the others? Hortense, and Louise, and Barbara? How will they fare?'

He was thinking of his half-brothers, she
knew, and she told him, without rancour,
'They feathered their nests whilst the King

lived. They'll go abroad now. Life won't change much, for them.'

'Well, we've my property in the north, and the money my court offices bring in. We shan't starve, mother.'

Before Nell could reply they heard footsteps outside the door, there was a brief tap on the wood, and James entered the room.

Nell stared, then faltered 'God save your Majesty,' and thought incredulously how unkingly he looked, with his eyes red-rimmed from grief and his mouth pursed with small importance.

'I've come to tell you, Nellie, that you need not worry about your debts,' he said breathlessly. 'I could not reach you at the palace, and then my man said you'd taken the boy home. My brother's last words were of you, my dear, and I shall never forget that.'

She found she could not speak, but looked her enquiry.

James cleared his throat, glancing at the boy. 'The King made his peace with God, and bade his sons and the Queen goodbye,' he said at last. 'He did not mention the ... the others. But just before he stopped breathing, he spoke of you, quite distinctly. And you may be sure I could never ignore my brother's last wish, even if it was not my own also. You shall be looked after.'

He smiled with difficulty at them, his grief still struggling to master him, and turned to go but Nell said impetuously, 'Oh, Sir! Your Majesty, I should say. Please tell me what Charles said?'

He turned again in the doorway. 'He cared for you deeply, you know. He motioned me to stand close and as I bent over the bed he whispered, "Don't let poor Nellie starve".'

# What Happened Later

Nell did not starve, for James kept his promise to Charles and paid off many of her debts, beside giving her a generous pension which he continued to pay her annually until her death, two years after Charles's. The pension was then paid to her son, St Albans.

During the first month or two after Charles's death, however, Nell *was* outlawed for debt; this must have been because her creditors took fright upon hearing of the King's death, for she speedily came into possession of money to pay her bills with. James wasted as little time as possible in coming to her aid, no matter how difficult the times were for him personally.

Nell died some time in November, 1687, 'of an apoplexy', and her body was buried, at her request, at the church of St Martin'sin-the-fields. Her will, which is still extant, is detailed and thoughtful, proving, it would seem, that she died only after a fairly lengthy illness during which she gave considerable attention to the will.

Rose outlived her, as did her son, the Duke of St Albans. He married Lady Diana de Vere and lived until 1726.